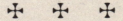

Dear Diary

The stars and my family align to make my life black and miserable. My mother seeks to make me a fine lady—dumb, docile and accomplished—so I must take lady-lessons and keep my mouth closed. My father, the toad, conspires to sell me like cheese to some lack-wit seeking a wife.

What makes this clodpole suitor anxious to have me? I am no beauty, being sun-browned and gray-eyed, with poor eyesight and a stubborn disposition.

Corpus bones! He comes to dine with us in two days' time. I plan to cross my eyes and drool in my meat.

✛ ✛ ✛

Critical Acclaim for
CATHERINE, CALLED BIRDY

CATHERINE, CALLED BIRDY

✠ ✠ ✠

BY KAREN CUSHMAN

📕 HarperTrophy®
An Imprint of HarperCollinsPublishers

Harper Trophy® is a registered trademark of
HarperCollins Publishers Inc.

Catherine, Called Birdy
Text copyright © 1994 by Karen Cushman
Printed in the United States of America. For information address
HarperCollins Children's Books, a division of HarperCollins Publishers,
1350 Avenue of the Americas, New York, NY 10019.

Reprinted by arrangement with Clarion Books,
a Houghton Mifflin Company imprint.

LC Number 93-23333

Trophy ISBN 0-06-440584-2
ISBN 0-06-073942-8 (special ed. pbk.)

First Harper Trophy edition, 1995
Visit us on the World Wide Web!
www.harperchildrens.com

✠

*This book is dedicated to Leah,
Danielle, Megan, Molly, Pamela,
and Tama, and to the imagination, hope,
and tenacity of all young women*

✠

# SEPTEMBER ✝

12TH DAY OF SEPTEMBER

I am commanded to write an account of my days: I am bit by fleas and plagued by family. That is all there is to say.

13TH DAY OF SEPTEMBER

My father must suffer from ale head this day, for he cracked me twice before dinner instead of once. I hope his angry liver bursts.

14TH DAY OF SEPTEMBER

Tangled my spinning again. Corpus bones, what a torture.

15TH DAY OF SEPTEMBER

Today the sun shone and the villagers sowed hay, gathered apples, and pulled fish from the stream. I, trapped inside, spent two hours embroidering a cloth for the church and three hours picking out my stitches after my mother saw it. I wish I were a villager.

16TH DAY OF SEPTEMBER
Spinning. Tangled.

17TH DAY OF SEPTEMBER
Untangled.

18TH DAY OF SEPTEMBER
If my brother Edward thinks that writing this account of my days will help me grow less childish and more learned, *he* will have to write it. I will do this no longer. And I will not spin. And I will not eat. Less childish indeed.

19TH DAY OF SEPTEMBER
I am delivered! My mother and I have made a bargain. I may forgo spinning as long as I write this account for Edward. My mother is not much for writing but has it in her heart to please Edward, especially now he is gone to be a monk, and I would do worse things to escape the foolish boredom of spinning. So I will write.

What follows will be my book—the book of Catherine, called Little Bird or Birdy, daughter of Rollo and the lady Aislinn, sister to Thomas, Edward, and the abominable Robert, of the village of Stonebridge in the shire of Lincoln, in the country of

England, in the hands of God. Begun this 19th day of September in the year of Our Lord 1290, the fourteenth year of my life. The skins are my father's, left over from the household accounts, and the ink also. The writing I learned of my brother Edward, but the words are my own.

Picked off twenty-nine fleas today.

20TH DAY OF SEPTEMBER

Today I chased a rat about the hall with a broom and set the broom afire, ruined my embroidery, threw it in the privy, ate too much for dinner, hid in the barn and sulked, teased the littlest kitchen boy until he cried, turned the mattresses, took the linen outside for airing, hid from Morwenna and her endless chores, ate supper, brought in the forgotten linen now wet with dew, endured scolding and slapping from Morwenna, pinched Perkin, and went to bed. And having writ this, Edward, I feel no less childish or more learned than I was.

21ST DAY OF SEPTEMBER

Something is astir. I can feel my father's eyes following me about the hall, regarding me as he would a new warhorse or a bull bought for breeding. I am surprised that he has not asked to examine my hooves.

And he asks me questions, the beast who never speaks to me except with the flat of his hand to my cheek or my rump.

This morning: "Exactly how old are you, daughter?"

This forenoon: "Have you all your teeth?"

"Is your breath sweet or foul?"

"Are you a good eater?"

"What color is your hair when it is clean?"

Before supper: "How are your sewing and your bowels and your conversation?"

What is brewing here?

Sometimes I miss my brothers, even the abominable Robert. With Robert and Thomas away in the king's service and Edward at his abbey, there are fewer people about for my father to bother, so he mostly fixes upon me.

22ND DAY OF SEPTEMBER

I am a prisoner to my needle again today, hemming linen in the solar with my mother and her women. This chamber is pleasant, large and sunny, with my mother and father's big bed on one side and, on the other, a window that looks out on the world I could be enjoying were I not in here sewing. I can see across the yard, past the stables and privy and cowshed, to the river and the gatehouse, over the fields to the village beyond. Cottages line the dusty road leading to the church at the far end. Dogs and geese and children tumble in play while the villagers plough. Would I were tumbling—or even ploughing—with them.

Here in my prison my mother works and gossips

with her women as if she didn't mind being chained to needle and spindle. My nurse Morwenna, now that I am near grown and not in need of her nursing, tortures me with complaints about the length of my stitches and the colors of my silk and the thumbprints on the altar cloth I am hemming.

If I had to be born a lady, why not a *rich* lady, so someone else could do the work and I could lie on a silken bed and listen to a beautiful minstrel sing while my servants hemmed? Instead I am the daughter of a country knight with but ten servants, seventy villagers, no minstrel, and acres of unhemmed linen. It grumbles my guts. I do not know what the sky is like today or whether the berries have ripened. Has Perkin's best goat dropped her kid yet? Did Wat the Farrier finally beat Sym at wrestling? I do not know. I am trapped here inside hemming.

Morwenna says it is the altar cloth for me. Corpus bones!

23RD DAY OF SEPTEMBER

There was a hanging in Riverford today. I am being punished for impudence again, so was not allowed to go. I am near fourteen and have never yet seen a hanging. My life is barren.

24TH DAY OF SEPTEMBER

The stars and my family align to make my life black and miserable. My mother seeks to make me a fine lady—dumb, docile, and accomplished—so I must take lady-lessons and keep my mouth closed. My brother Edward thinks even girls should not be ignorant, so he taught me to read holy books and to write, even though I would rather sit in an apple tree and wonder. Now my father, the toad, conspires to sell me like a cheese to some lack-wit seeking a wife.

What makes this clodpole suitor anxious to have me? I am no beauty, being sun-browned and gray-eyed, with poor eyesight and a stubborn disposition. My family holds but two small manors. We have plenty of cheese and apples but no silver or jewels or boundless acres to attract a suitor.

Corpus bones! He comes to dine with us in two days' time. I plan to cross my eyes and drool in my meat.

26TH DAY OF SEPTEMBER

Master Lack-Wit comes today, despite my mother's objections. Although she is wed to a knight of no significance, her fathers were kings in Britain long ago, she says. And my suitor is but a wool merchant from Great Yarmouth who aspires to be mayor and thinks a wife with noble relations, no matter how distant, will be an advantage.

My father bellowed, "Sweet Judas, lady, think you we can eat your royal ancestors or plant your family name? The man stinks of gold. If he will have her and pay well for the privilege, your daughter will be a wife."

When there is money involved, my father can be quite well spoken.

THE HOUR OF VESPERS, LATER THIS DAY: My suitor has come and gone. The day was gray and drippy so I sat in the privy to watch him arrive. I thought it well to know my enemy.

Master Lack-Wit was of middle years and fashionably pale. He was also a mile high and bony as a herring, with gooseberry eyes, chin like a hatchet, and tufts of orange hair sprouting from his head, his ears, and his nose. And all his ugliness came wrapped in glorious robes of samite and ermine that fell to big red leather boots. It put me in mind of the time I put my mother's velvet cap and veil on Perkin's granny's rooster.

Hanging on to the arm of Rhys from the stables, for the yard was slippery with rain and horse droppings and chicken dung, he greeted us: "Good fordood to you, by lord, and to you, Lady Aislidd. I ab hodored to bisit your bodest badder and beet the baided."

I thought first he spoke in some foreign tongue or a cipher designed to conceal a secret message, but it seems only that his nose was plugged. And it stayed plugged throughout his entire visit, while he breathed and chewed and chattered through his open mouth. Corpus bones! He troubled my stomach no little bit and I determined to rid us of him this very day.

I rubbed my nose until it shone red, blacked out my front teeth with soot, and dressed my hair with the mouse bones I found under the rushes in the hall. All through dinner, while he talked of his warehouses stuffed with greasy wool and the pleasures of the annual Yarmouth herring fair, I smiled my gaptooth smile at him and wiggled my ears.

My father's crack still rings my head but Master Lack-Wit left without a betrothal.

27TH DAY OF SEPTEMBER

Being imprisoned in the solar was none so bad this day, for I heard welcome gossip. My uncle George is coming home. Near twenty years ago he went crusading with Prince Edward. Edward came home to be king but George stayed, finding other lords to serve. My mother says he is brave and honorable. My father says he is woolly-witted. Morwenna, who was nurse to my mother before me, just sighs and winks at me.

Since my uncle George has had experience with adventures, I am hoping that he can help me escape this life of hemming and mending and fishing for husbands. I would much prefer crusading, swinging my sword at heathens and sleeping under starry skies on the other end of the world.

I told all this to the cages of birds in my chamber and they listened quite politely. I began to keep birds in order to hear their chirping, but most often now they have to listen to mine.

28TH DAY OF SEPTEMBER, *Michaelmas Eve*

Perkin says that in the village of Woodford near Lincoln a man has grown a cabbage that looks like the head of Saint Peter the Apostle. People are gathering from all over the shire to pray and wonder at it. My mother, of course, will not let me go. I had thought to ask Saint Peter to strengthen my eyes, for I know it unattractive to squint as I do. And to make my father forget this marriage business.

29TH DAY OF SEPTEMBER, *Michaelmas, Feast of the Archangel Michael*

Last night the villagers lit the Michaelmas bonfires and set two cottages and a haystack afire. Cob the Smith and Beryl, John At-Wood's daughter, were in the haystack. They are scorched and sheepish but unhurt. They are also now betrothed.

Today is quarter-rent day. My greedy father is near muzzle-witted with glee from the geese, silver pennies, and wagonloads of manure our tenants pay him. He guzzles ale and slaps his belly, laughing as he gathers in the rents. I like to sit near the table where William the Steward keeps the record and listen to the villagers complain about my father as they pay. I have gotten all my good insults and best swear words that way.

Henry Newhouse always pays first, for at thirty acres his is the largest holding. Then come Thomas Baker, John Swann from the alehouse, Cob the Smith, Walter Mustard, and all the eighteen tenants down to Thomas Cotter and the widow Joan Proud, who hold no land but pay for their leaky cottages in turnips, onions, and goose grease.

Perkin the goat boy holds no land either, but pays a goat each year as rent for his grandmother's cottage. For weeks before Michaelmas, Perkin tells everyone in the village, "I will pay him any goat, but not the black one" or "not the gray one." William Steward of course hears and tells my father, and come rent day my father insists on the black one or the gray one that Perkin did not wish to part with. My father gloats and thinks he is getting the best of Perkin, but Perkin always winks at me as he leaves. And each year the goat my father demands is the weakest or the meanest or the one that eats the laundry off the line or the rushes off the floor. Perkin is the cleverest person I know.

30TH DAY OF SEPTEMBER

Morwenna says when I have done with writing, I must help with the soap-making. The bubbling mess stinks worse than the privy in summer. Therefore I plan to write abundantly.

First, I will say more about Perkin. Although he is the goat boy, Perkin is my good friend and heart's brother. He is very thin and goodly-looking, with golden hair and blue eyes just like the king, but is much dirtier than the king although much cleaner than the other villagers. He is sore afflicted with wind in his bowels, so I regularly make him a tonic of cumin seed and anise to unbind his liver and destroy the wind. It mostly does not work.

One of his legs is considerably shorter than the other, so as he walks he seems to be dancing some graceless dance, with his head bobbing and arms swinging about to keep his balance. Once I tied a bucket on my foot so I could walk like Perkin and we could dance together, but my arms and legs quickly grew tired. Perkin must be tired all the time, but it doesn't make him ill-tempered.

He lives with the goats or his granny, depending on the season, and is mostly wise and kind when he isn't teasing me. It is Perkin who taught me to name the birds, to know the weather from the sky, to spit between my front teeth, to cheat at draughts and not get caught, all the most important things I know, the Devil take sewing and spinning.

I am frequently told not to spend so much time with the goat boy, so of course I seek him out whenever I can. Once I came upon him in the field, chewing on a grass, saying some words over and over to himself.

"What spell are you casting, witch-boy?" I asked.

"No spell," said he, "but the Norman and Latin words for apple, which I lately heard and am saying over and over so I do not forget."

Perkin likes things like that. He would like to be learned. When he discovers new words, he uses them all together: "This apple/*pomme*/*malus* is not ripe" or "Sometimes goats/*chevres*/*capri* are smarter than people." Some people have trouble understanding Perkin, but I know always what is in his heart.

My hand grows tired and I am out of ink and Morwenna is sending me black looks. I fear it is the soap-making for me. Am I doomed to spend my days stirring great vats of goose fat when not writing for Edward?

I wonder why rubbing your face and hands with black and sandy evil-smelling soap makes them clean. Why doesn't it just make them black and sandy? There is no more to say.

# October ✠

1ST DAY OF OCTOBER

My father's clerk suffers today from an inflammation of his eyes, caused, no doubt, by his spying on our serving maids as they wash under their arms at the millpond. I did not have the mother's milk necessary for an ointment for the eyes, so I used garlic and goose fat left from doctoring Morwenna's boils yesterweek. No matter how he bellowed, it will do him no harm.

I can stand no more of lady-tasks, endless mindless sewing, hemming, brewing, doctoring, and counting linen! Why is a lady too gentle to climb a tree or throw stones into the river when it is lady's work to pick maggots from the salt meat? Why must I learn to walk with a lady's tiny steps one day and sweat over great steaming kettles of dung and nettle for remedies the next? Why must the lady of the manor do all the least lovable tasks? I'd rather be the pig boy.

There are Jews in our hall tonight! On their way to London, they sought shelter from the rain. My father being away, my mother let them in. She is not afraid of Jews, but the cook and the kitchen boys have all fled to the barn, so no one will have supper tonight. I plan to hide in the shadows of the hall in order to see their horns and tails. Wait until Perkin hears of this.

THE HOUR OF VESPERS, LATER THIS DAY: Bones! The Jews have no horns and no tails, just wet clothes and ragged children. They are leaving England by order of the king, who says Jews are Hell-born, wicked, and dangerous. He must know some others than the scared and scrawny ones who are here this night.

I hid in the hall to watch them, hoping to see them talk to the Devil or perform evil deeds. But the men just drank and sang and argued and waved their arms about while the women chattered among themselves. Much like Christians. The children mostly snuffled and whined until one woman with a face like a withered apple gathered them about her. At first she spoke to them in the Jews' tongue, which sounds much like horses talking, but then with a wink in my direction she changed to English.

First she told of an old man named Abraham who actually argued with God and had great adventures in the desert. Then Moses, who I recognized from the Bible but forgot was a Jew. The woman said Moses led the Jews from a land of slavery to freedom, just as they were going to find freedom in Flanders, riding in tall ships with billowing sails, pushed on by the breath of God.

Then she told a story about this man who was so stupid that he forgot how to get dressed in the morning. Where was his shirt? Did it go on his legs or his arms? And how did it fasten? Such trouble it was every morning. Finally he decided to hire the boy next door to come in each day and tell him, "Your shoes are there and your cloak is here and your hat goes on your head." The first day the boy comes in. "First," he says to the stupid man, "wash yourself." "That's all very well," says the stupid man, "but where is myself? Where in the world am I? Am I here? Am I here? Or am I here?" And he looked under the bed and behind the chair and in the street, but it was all in vain for he never did find himself.

As she spoke, the children stopped their snuffling and chanted with her, "Am I here? Or am I here?" And then shyly they began to shove each other and giggle, wiping their runny noses on their sleeves and skirts.

"Listen to me, my children," said the old woman then, "do not be like the stupid man. Know where you yourself are. How? By knowing who you are and where you come from. Just as a river by night shines with the reflected light of the moon, so too do you shine with the light of your family, your people, and

✣ 15 ✣

your God. So you are never far from home, never alone, wherever you go."

It was a wonder. She was like a minstrel, or a magician spinning stories from her wrinkled mouth. And then she pulled from the sleeves of her gown bread and onions and herring and boiled cabbage and they ate. One tiny little girl with soft eyes brought me an onion and some bread. Mayhap I wasn't hidden as well as I thought. It smelled like our food and I was hungry from hearing of the adventures of Moses, so I ate it. I did not die nor turn into a Jew. I think some stories are true and some stories are just stories.

4TH DAY OF OCTOBER

I was unhappy to see the Jews leave this morning until I got it in my mind to travel with them and have an experience, mayhap even find my own way in the world and never return to old Spinning and Sewing Manor. I wore an old tunic and leggings of Edward's, stuffed my hair into a cap, swaggered and spit, and looked much like a boy, except that I was curiously flat between the legs. I had thought to stuff the leggings with straw but feared that would make it hard to walk, so I went as I was. I could hear my nurse Morwenna calling for me as we left, but she never thought to look at the boy in the wool cap.

I walked with them all the way to Wooton-under-Wynwoode, hoping to hear more stories, but the old woman was silent. Instead I told her about my life and the boredom of sewing and brewing and doctoring and how I would rather go crusading like Uncle George or live with the goats like Perkin. Then, stroking my face with her rough hands, she said, "Little Bird, in the world to come, you will not be asked 'Why were you not George?' or 'Why were you not Perkin?' but 'Why were you not Catherine?' "

What did that mean? She said no more, so finally, confused and more than a little sad, I left them for the Wooton harvest fair. It was not much of a fair, but they did have a ribbon seller, an ale tent, a stilt-walker, and a two-headed goat.

I had never been so far from home without Morwenna. It felt like a bit of an adventure. I examined a wagon with copper-banded barrels, knives, ropes, and needles for sale. I watched two men argue over the value of a cow who just looked tired and puzzled and ready to go home. I saw three small boys stealing mouthfuls of ale from a keg behind the ale tent, laughing and spluttering and pretending to be drunk.

Down behind the horse auction was a small stage where a little wooden Noah and his wife danced on strings, while God ordered Noah to build an ark and Mrs. Noah, pulling angrily at her husband's coat, scolded him about finishing his chores and not expecting her to get on that flimsy boat.

Finally Noah wrestled his wife, grown quite peevish, to the ground amid shouts of "Cry mercy, I say!" and "Never! I say nay!" until finally they lay in a heap of tangled strings.

Then came the grand procession of the animals—
two by two—on a painted scroll, unwound by the
puppeteer and his apprentice so the animals looked
to be crossing the stage, full alive and lively, as Noah
called,

> *Lions come in, and leopards, and dogs,*
> *Barnyard creatures, goats and hogs,*
> *Chickens, turkeys, all feathered fowl,*
> *Hairy beasts that bark and that howl!*

When the ark was loaded, it rode out a silver gilt
rain on a sea of blue-green satin until the dove de-
scended on golden strings to promise land and life to
all. It was a glorious spectacle, even though I could
see the puppeteer's apprentice throughout, pulling
strings and banging pots and wiping his nose on the
curtain.

It was then that William Steward, at the fair to
purchase barrels, saw me and threatened to pull me
by my hair all the way home. Being right hungry, I
went with him most willingly, in exchange for his
promise to say nothing about my adventure. On our
way out, we passed baskets of cocks for the cock-
fight. Looking as innocent as I was able, I kicked the
baskets over and the cocks escaped. Deus! I thought
I was Moses leading them to freedom and home to
their wives and baby chicks. Instead, they flew at
each other with their terrible sharpened claws,
shrieking and slashing in a storm of feathers.

I had had enough of that fair and was ready to go home. I told my mother and Morwenna that I'd spent the day sulking in the dovecote. They believed me. It is something I would do.

5TH DAY OF OCTOBER

The cook's boy told me today of a miller's apprentice in Nottingham who can fart at will. That, I think, is a useful and notable talent, to the Devil with spinning. I purposely ate too much dinner and tried to see if I had the talent. I don't.

6TH DAY OF OCTOBER

This being Saint Faith's day, Morwenna and I chased the cook out of the kitchen so that we could bake a Saint Faith's cake. I passed pieces of it through my mother's ruby ring and have hung the ring from my bedstead. Tonight Saint Faith will send a dream of who my husband will be. I should be pleased if he is a prince or a knight with golden hair. Or a juggler in ruby silk tunic and purple tights. Or a wandering minstrel with music in his throat and mischief in his eye.

7TH DAY OF OCTOBER

Dreamed of the miller's farting apprentice. This morning I stomped the cake into the rushes on the floor and threw the ring into the pig yard. I will never marry.

8TH DAY OF OCTOBER

Searched the pig yard for my mother's ring until dark. Have definitely decided not to be a pig boy.

9TH DAY OF OCTOBER

I am well pleased with the events of today and have celebrated with a handful of blackberries and the rest of the pork pie from supper. As I eat, I will recount the day so as to relive the pleasure. This morning, from the window of the solar, I could hear the villagers singing and shouting as they went about building a cottage for Ralph Littlemouse, who lost his in the Michaelmas celebrations. Poor me, I thought. Trapped inside again. Missing all the merriment. But then my mother, who was looking a little green in her face, curled up on her great bed and pulled the curtains close about her. And Morwenna went to the kitchen to argue with the cook about dinner. So down the stairs I went, skidding through the hall and across the yard, down the road to the village, tucking up my skirts and pulling off my shoes as I ran.

Already this early they had the framework of the cottage up, and Joan Proud, Marjorie Mustard, and Ralph's children were weaving willow sticks through to make the walls.

Nearby, in a hollow in the ground, my favorite part of building was beginning and I jumped right in, mucking about to mix the puddle of mud, straw, cow hair, and dung into daub for covering the walls. The slop felt delightful, squishing through my toes. The sun was shining, breezes blowing, the blackberries were ripe, people were singing "Hey nonny nonny" and "There was a maiden good and fair," and I had muck between my toes. Oh, to be a villager.

Then I had my first good idea. I scooped up a handfill of muck and flung it in the air, watching it land *plop* and *sloop* on the faces, arms, and shoulders of my fellow muckers. Handfuls of the gray and stinking stuff came back at me and I had to fling more and they had to fling more until we all looked like plaster saints and not like people at all.

Suddenly everything stopped—no singing, no flinging, no weaving of willows. All eyes were on a young man standing in the road, holding the bridle of the most beautiful horse I've ever seen. The young man was beautiful, too, with golden hair and golden eyes and a tunic of gold and green velvet. No one spoke, but as I was right curious, I walked up to him.

"Good morning, sir. Can I assist you?" I asked, very nicely for me.

He stared at me long without speaking, while his forehead furrowed and his mouth grew small as a mouse's turd. Finally he replied, "My God, the stink! Is there no water for washing or scent for covering up in this village?"

I said nothing. I didn't think he really wanted an answer.

He went on, "Is that ahead the manor of Rollo of Stonebridge?"

"What do you want with the lord Rollo?" I asked.

"It be none of your business, maid, but I am inspecting the family with an eye to marrying the daughter Catherine," he replied, taking a piece of scent-drenched linen from his sleeve and holding it to his nose.

Corpus bones, I thought. To be wedded to this perfumed prig with his mouth in a knot and a frown always on his face! That is when I had my next very good idea.

"The lady Catherine," I repeated, trying to sound like a villager. "Oh, good fortune to ye, good sir. Ye sorely will need it."

"I will? Is aught amiss with the lady?"

"No, sir. Oh, no. She is a goodly lady, given that her wits are lacking and her back stooped. Mostly she is gentle and quiet, when she is not locked up. And the pits on her face are much better now. Truly. Please, sir, never say I suggested the lady Catherine was lacking. Please, sir."

I made then to grab his arm but he twisted away, leapt onto the back of the beautiful horse, and was off on the road toward the manor. Bones! I thought. He is still going on! But as I watched, the beautiful horse with the beautiful young man left the road, made a wide turn in the field, trampling the carefully seeded furrows of Walter Mustard, and tore off away from the manor, away from my father, and, thanks be, away from me.

All during supper my father watched the door, finally pondering aloud about the whereabouts of someone named Rolf, which I of course did not know. So this is why I am pleased with today, and pork pie seems not great enough celebration for what I have saved myself from.

10TH DAY OF OCTOBER

Just three days to the feast of Saint Edward, my brother Edward's saint's day. When Edward was still at home, we celebrated this day each year with feasting and dancing and mock battles in the yard. Now our celebrations include my father's face turning purple, my mother tightening her eyes and her mouth, and the cook swinging his ladle and swearing in Saxon. The cause of all the excitement is this: On this day each year, since Edward went to be a monk, my mother takes wagons full of gifts to his abbey in his honor. My father shouts that we may as well pour his precious stores in the cesspit (one day his angry liver will set him afire and I will toast bread on him). My mother calls him Pinch-Fist and Miser. The cook boils and snarls as his bacon and flour and Rhenish wine leave home. But each year my mother stands firm and the wagons go. This year we send:

460 salted white herring
3 wheels of cheese, a barrel of apples
4 chickens, 3 ducks, and 87 pigeons
4 barrels of flour, honey from our bees

100 gallons of ale (for no one drinks more ale
    than monks, my father says)
4 iron pots, wooden spoons, and a rat trap for
    the kitchen
goose fat for the making of everyday candles
    and soap (lots of candles and little soap,
    I wager, seeing that they are monks)
40 pounds of beeswax for candles for the
    church
a chest of blankets, linens, and napkins
horn combs, for those who have hair
goose quills, down, and a bolt of woven cloth
    (black)

My mother longs to see Edward on this day each
year. He is her favorite child. No small wonder. Robert
is abominable and I puzzle that she had any more
children after bearing him first. I would have exposed
him by the river. Thomas has been gone so long with
the king that we hardly know him. I am stubborn,
peevish, and as prickly as a thistle. So by default alone
Edward would be her favorite. And mine.

11TH DAY OF OCTOBER

Last night my mother lost the child she carried,
the fifth I have seen die without ever having a
chance to live. If God intends for me to be her last, I
wish He would stop quickening her and then taking
the baby away. She mourns so. I do not believe God
means to punish my mother, who may not be learned

✠ 24 ✠

or clever but is mostly good. I think He is just not paying enough attention.

White-faced, she lies in her big bed in the solar while Morwenna gives her goblets of garlic and mint and vinegar to cleanse her womb, and soothes her with "Oh my poor lady"s and clucking sounds. I must go with the wagons in her place and see Edward tomorrow—more learning to be the lady of the manor. Deus! The road is rough, the weather hot, the monks old and smelly. We leave after breakfast and hope to be well on the way before the sun finds us.

12TH DAY OF OCTOBER

No more sewing and spinning and goose fat for me! Today my life is changed. How it came about is this: We arrived at the abbey soon after dinner, stopping just outside the entry gate at the guesthouse next the mill. The jouncing cart did my stomach no kindness after jellied eel and potted lamb, so I was most relieved to alight.

A tall monk with a big nose greeted us and led us from the guesthouse through the abbey gate, past kitchens and dormitories and vast storehouses, to the abbot's office behind the chapel.

The abbot received us kindly and sent to my mother gentle words and a marvelous small book of saints, their feast days, and their great works. Today, it says, is the feast of Saint Edwin, the first Christian king of Northumbria, whose head lies at York and body in the abbey at Whitby. I think there are too many words and not enough pictures, but since I read and my mother does not, I will try to seduce it from her.

Brother Anselm, the big-nosed monk, then escorted me to Edward's desk in the writing room. Women are not allowed in ordinarily, but I believe they think me not quite a woman yet.

Edward works in Paradise. Beyond the garden, near the chapel, is a room as large as our barn and near as cold. Shelves lining the walls hold books and scrolls, some chained down as if they were precious relics or wild beasts. In three rows sit fifteen desks, feebly lit by candles, and fifteen monks sit curled over them, their noses pressed almost to the desktops. Each monk holds in one hand his pen and in the other a sharp knife for scratching out mistakes. On the desks are pens and quills of all sizes, pots of ink black or colored, powder for drying, and knives for sharpening.

Some of the monks copy the words from one page to another. Others add fanciful designs to the first letter and decoration to the page. Still others punch holes in the pages and sew them together between wooden covers. Never have I seen books so beautiful or so plentiful.

The monks didn't talk to me much or even listen to me much, but they didn't send me away. I visited Brother William who was mixing colors and gave him some good ideas for inks—a rose the color of a newborn lamb's nose and the iridescent green you sometimes see in the film inside a fresh raw egg. He said nothing, only snorted, but I am sure he was grateful for these suggestions.

Another monk let me help prepare the vellum for the next day's writing, but I knew the skins came from our sheep and I was afraid I would recognize one. I have the same feeling when the cook stuffs swans and geese and lambs whole and sets them before us at special feasts. I preferred smoothing and powdering the vellum pages after they looked less like animals, even though the powder got into my hair and my nose and my clothes.

Edward's passion is for the letters and the words, which he inscribes lovingly on the softened vellum. But for me—oh, the pictures! The birds and the flowers, the saints and angels rushing up the side of the page, climbing over the capitals and down the margin, the knights riding snails into battle against squirrels and goats, the many faces of the Devil as he scampers over the page, tempting the reader away from the holy words. To spend the rest of my life making pictures instead of mending and weaving would be Heaven indeed!

That is when my life changed. I decided to run away to an abbey. This is how I will live, making pictures in the scriptorium, although I wish the place were livelier. I know it will be difficult, given that I am a girl, but I am also stubborn and clever. The abbey cannot be this one, as much as I would love to be near Edward, for they know me here and know I am no boy. I must find another, close enough for visits from Perkin, with a writing room and mayhap an aged abbot who doesn't see too well.

Do brothers see each other naked? Who would know if a new brother were a maid and no brother at all? I must find out. Would Edward tell me? Tomorrow when I take my leave of him, I will ask.

Tonight we sleep at the guesthouse. It is near enough to the abbey so I can practice being a monk. I wonder what monks do.

13TH DAY OF OCTOBER, *Feast of Edward, King and saint, and my brother Edward's saint's day*

A big difference between Robert and Edward is how they laugh at me. Robert laughs loudly, showing his big yellow horse teeth, pinching and slapping my cheeks. Edward laughs softly and kindly, but laugh he does. And did. He said with these apples on my chest, I would not fool even the most aged of abbots. Deus! Last year they were but walnuts and I might have gotten away with it.

I thought mayhap to join a nunnery instead, but as the chief occupation of nuns is embroidery, it would be like falling from the spit into the cooking fire. I could grow turnips, but I have neither land nor seeds. Be a tumbler, but I do not tumble, except when I am trying not to. A musician, but I do not play. I used to study music, since my mother said a lady must be accomplished, but the noise I made was so awful my father gave my lute to the cook. I could be a traveling spinner, but that is no escape. I am left with a beastly father, a life of chores, no hope, no friends, no escape, and a large bosom! Corpus bones! Is there no justice in the world?

14TH DAY OF OCTOBER, *Feast of Saint Callistus, slave, banker, convict, pope, and martyr*

My mother must give me the little book of saints. I am already making use of it to find how saints lived and died and what lessons I may learn from them.

On the way home from the abbey we stopped at Highgate Manor to bring greetings to the Baron Ranulf's family, who are visiting there until Christmas. Their daughter, Lady Aelis, and I were together at Belleford long ago, learning highborn manners and the duties of a lady, until my mother lost another of my unborn baby brothers and in sorrow called me home. What I remember most about Aelis is she liked to complain, said "Yes, my lady" and "No, my lord" but did as she pleased when no one could see, and was more fun than anyone else.

She has been living of late at the French court. I watched her at supper. She looks to be a lady with her fancy French table manners and her yellow hair, but during the dancing she grabbed my arm and pulled me from the hall for a gossip. We tucked up our skirts and walked round and round the dark manor yard arm in arm, talking of who has rotten teeth and who married someone rich and ugly and who paints her face and stuffs her bosom.

We flirted with the guards and arranged to meet them later in a chamber, where we will send Aelis's old nurse and her sewing woman on some pretext. They will all have a surprise. Aelis told me she gets away with things because she looks so docile and innocent while she does just what she wants. She says she would like to be a horse trainer but knows she was brought home to wed. It appears that we are both in grave danger of being sold like pigs at autumn fair.

We pledged to meet in seven days' time at the high meadow, it being but half a day's walk for each of us. Since I left Belleford I have not been much with other girls, and I long to tell her of my life and thoughts and wonderings and hear hers.

15TH DAY OF OCTOBER, *Feast of Saint Euthymius the Younger, who lived three years on nuts and herbs*

Home again. While hiding from Morwenna before supper, I watched the geese returning from the pasture to their shed in the yard, all in a line like plump little knights in feathers.

I think I love geese more than any other birds because no one else does. They are not small and delicate like larks and sparrows, or swift and clever like hawks and falcons. They do not sing like nightingales and cannot be trained to talk or dance or do tricks. They are cunning, greedy, shortsighted, and stubborn—much like me, now that I think on it.

I have seen swans on the river. They are much

more beautiful and stately than geese, but a little vain and not as smart. I think my mother is like a swan. My brother Robert is a rooster, strutting here and there, crowing about himself. Edward is a heron, with his long nose and long legs. Clever Perkin is a falcon, and my nurse Morwenna is a nuthatch, busy and brown and dumpy. My father of course is a buzzard, slow and stupid, the Devil take him. I think perhaps Aelis is a dove on the outside and a hawk within. And I am a plain gray and brown goose.

16TH DAY OF OCTOBER, *Feast of Saint Helwig, who was unlucky in her children*

Before I left the abbey, Edward showed me how to mix some colors and shape goose feathers into pens so I too can make flowers and angels. The black ink is easy. We have walnut husks and an abundance of soot. I also found buttercups, sneezeweed, and moss for yellows and greens, but have no lapis lazuli stone to grind for blue. I made a paste from crushed bilberries that looks as blue as a robin's egg but grows sour and so sticky that I must add a task the brothers never dreamed of—picking bugs out of the heavenly sky or the Virgin's veil.

17TH DAY OF OCTOBER, *Feasts of Saints Ethelred and Ethelbricht, sons of Ermenred, great-grandsons of Ethelbert, brothers of Ermenburga, nephews of Erconbert, and cousins of Egbert*

I had a sweet dream last night. In my dream I

was captured by a dragon who looked like my father. My uncle George, wearing a cloak made of feathers, stabbed the dragon in the neck with a goose-quill pen. Then George leapt onto his horse and, reaching down, gathered me up and lifted me to his lap. We rode off together to be crusaders. After I awoke, I kept my eyes closed for a long time so I could hold on to the dream.

18TH DAY OF OCTOBER, *Feast of Saint Luke, writer of gospels, physician, and artist, who lived to be eighty-four and died unmarried*

In the village late last night, one of Thomas Cotter's chickens, hunting in the dirt of the cottage floor for bugs, scratched too close to the cooking fire and set her feathers aflame. She squawked and flapped about the cottage, from bed to table to the bacon hanging from the roof beams, setting all on fire. Chased by a naked Thomas, the chicken flew out the door and down the road toward the church, leaving little fires smoldering in her path, until Ralph Littlemouse threw a bucket of water on her, whereupon she lay down gasping in the road, bald and charred. Thomas's family now sleep in our hall until a new cottage is built—all the family but the chicken, which they ate. I try not to laugh when I see Thomas's family, for they are sore grieved. It is no easy task.

The king, I think, should be informed of this event. I can see him besieging the Scots by setting fire to hundreds of chickens and letting them flap over the Scottish castle walls.

19TH DAY OF OCTOBER, *Feast of Saint Frileswide, virgin, though why that should make someone a saint I do not know*

While we picked bugs and burrs from the weaving wool this morning, Morwenna tried to make me understand why my father seeks a husband for me and why it is my duty to marry where he says. I understand full well. He is as greedy as a goat.

I believe we have enough of things. Those with many manors have to travel from one to another to take care of them. More cows and pigs mean more dung. More pots and bowls and tables mean more cooking and scrubbing. But my father does not see it my way and seeks to improve our position through my marriage bed. Corpus bones. I have not even begun my monthly courses yet, so how can I be a wife?

Later I told Morwenna my jest about the flaming chickens and she, traitor and carrytale, told my mother. I have now to embroider another cloth for the church. They think I am not trying hard enough not to laugh. Bleak. All is bleak.

20TH DAY OF OCTOBER, *Feast of Saint Irene, killed by a man because she would not love him*

My uncle George has come home! He is tall and fair and funny. Last night he told us wondrous stories of the places he has been. The cities have names that whisper like the wind: Venice, Damascus, Byzantium, Samarkand. I say them over and over to myself so I will not forget them before I can tell Perkin. I used to imagine Uncle George in the Holy Land, wearing a red cross sewn on his white tunic, nobly fighting for God and Christ and England. I could almost see the line of crusaders reaching from Jerusalem all the way back to London, like a procession on a holy day or the arrival of foreign merchants at the fair, with snow-white horses and mules prancing in their bells and silks, ladies in coaches of gold and jewels gleaming in the sun like fire, musicians with harps and timbrels and trumpets, and little children scampering alongside throwing flowers in their path as they sing songs of praise to those coming to free them from the heathens. It must have been like the march of the righteous into Paradise.

I told Uncle George about my imaginings and he laughed and laughed. He said I did get one thing right: There were plenty of donkeys, but not all of them had four legs. His years on crusade, he said, were more like Hell than the Heaven I imagine, with little cheering and singing but much dying of thirst, eating dead horses, and wading knee-deep in blood and broken bodies. I must doubt this.

21ST DAY OF OCTOBER, *Feast of Saint Ursula and her eleven thousand companions, martyred by the Huns*
    Uncle George is teaching me—in Latin, Greek, and Arabic—what he says are the most useful

phrases for a crusader:

"Tell me the way again, more slowly."

"How much for wine? Too much."

"Have you herbs for my aching head?"

"You cheat. You lie. You son of a dog and a camel."

Mayhap Uncle George will help me take up the cross and be a crusader. I won't even have to bind my chest and pretend to be a man, for it is well known how Eleanor, wife of the second Henry, mother of Richard the Lionheart and the terrible John Softsword, led her band of women on crusade. They sat astride magnificent white horses and, below their linen tunics, wore tight-fitting hose and red leather boots to the knee with orange silk lining. I would *walk* to the Holy Land for red boots with orange silk lining. I will speak to Uncle George.

22ND DAY OF OCTOBER, *Feast of Saint Donatus, an Irish man who was proclaimed a bishop when bells miraculously rang as he entered church*

Learned men in the East call this the birthday of the world, the anniversary of the Creation on this day four thousand year ago. So says Uncle George. I wonder who has kept the reckoning. Few of the villagers know even when they were born. They say it was the year the miller's barn caught fire or the new priest was driven from the village for lechery.

Uncle George's baggage finally caught up with him and he has given us all presents—bronze knives and cooking pots, silk for my mother in shades of saffron and lavender, and for our stomachs ginger, cinnamon, cloves, figs, dates, and almonds. For me, something called an orange, shriveled and dry, with a brown musty smell. When I close my eyes, under the must I can smell just a hint of sweet hot sunshine. George says when they are new, oranges taste like water from the rivers of Paradise.

He also brought me a special gift, a popinjay in a cage carved of ivory and sweet-smelling wood, to join the family of birds in my chamber. Since my father built the solar where he and my mother and any important guests sleep, I share a sleeping chamber only with my nurse Morwenna, my mother's serving women, any visiting girls, and my birds. With the popinjay, I have nineteen birds in cages hanging from the roof timbers. Linnets, skylarks, and nightingales for their song, magpies for their talk. Now that I don't have to hear my father bellowing and snoring and spitting, I can hear their music. Last night I fell asleep smelling my orange and listening to my birds sing. I dreamed I was an angel.

23RD DAY OF OCTOBER, *Feast of Saint Cuthbert, first man ever to shoe a horse*

I was finally able to speak to Uncle George about my idea of going on crusade to the Holy Land. It is too late, he says. Their own greed, cruelty, and stupidity defeated the crusaders, and the Turks have only to sweep them out like soiled straw.

Sometimes George does not sound like one who

has worn the Holy Cross. He says he stopped being a crusader when he realized God could not be pleased by so much blood, no matter whose.

He makes me confused. My cheeks glow, my heart flutters like a hawk moth, and my dreams grow soft and swoony. I do not know if the turmoil of the liver I am suffering is because of George or because I had two portions of eel pie for supper.

24TH DAY OF OCTOBER, *Feast of Saint Maglorius, who chased a dragon out of Jersey*

I met Aelis in the high meadow, as we planned. She had lost the circlet that bound her hair, her boots were torn and muddy, and her nose was red from the sun. She looked much like me.

She told me more stories of the French king and his ladies, of castles and tournaments, of the Lady Ghislaine who kept a tame badger, of Guillot of Lyons who farted as he bowed to the king and was sent from court for a year, of her best friend Marie who married a ghost.

I told her about my handsome, confusing Uncle George. She is eager to see him for herself, so I will have my mother invite her for my saint's day celebration.

Aelis thinks George must look like the archangel Michael. I told her he looks more like the Saint George who slew the dragon. In truth he is handsomer than either of those, for his green eyes are alive and change colors in the sun, at times a red blush flows across his cheeks, tiny drops of sweat shine in the little hairs about his mouth, and he smells of horses and spice and leather. No dead saint could be as beautiful as that.

I missed dinner and supper both, but I reached home before dark. I told my mother I was gathering sloes for jelly for Morwenna. Told Morwenna I was sent for rose hips for my mother. Mayhap they will not compare stories until after I am asleep.

My uncle George is an eagle.

25TH DAY OF OCTOBER, *Feast of Saints Crispin and Crispinian, shoemakers, pricked to death with cobblers' awls*

I have mixed water and eggs with my writing inks to make paint for my chamber walls, where I am painting a scene from Heaven, with dogs and birds who look like me, angels with my mother's face, and saints with the faces of Edward and Aelis and George. Below is Hell, where poor souls with my father's face writhe in eternal torment. I gave God Perkin's face since Perkin is the wisest person I know, but Morwenna flew into a terrible fright, wailing about blasphemy and damnation, so I painted Perkin out and now God just has a sort of watery gray face.

26TH DAY OF OCTOBER, *Feast of Saints Eata and Bean, which I think is very funny*

Meg from the dairy and I sorted cider apples today. My mother makes the best cider in Lincolnshire. She swears it is because she always includes a number of rotten apples in the mix. I was wondering if this could be true of people—if the world needs a few rotten people to make the sweetest mix. This would explain the problem of God allowing evil in the world.

Meg only giggles when I talk to her of these matters. She is, however, good to talk to about how to get a weakly calf to drink from a pail, what will keep fairies from getting into your eggs, and whose wife threw him out of the cottage for taking too much ale. Except for Perkin, Meg is probably my best friend on the manor, when I can stop her from curtsying and my lady-ing me.

27TH DAY OF OCTOBER, *Feast of Saint Olran, over whose soul angels and devils fought*

The sun is shining, so I have thrown open the shutter in my chamber to let light and air in. I love my chamber when it is warm and sunny. In the middle is the bed I share with Morwenna, large and high, with curtains all around and a trundle under, where the serving maids sleep. At the foot is a chest, carved and dark with age, that looks as if it should be full of treasure but instead is stuffed with old clothes. On the right wall is my mural of Heaven and Hell. On the left wall are three pegs for my gowns and cloaks. And straight ahead is the window, shutters open now, and a stool pulled up, so I can sit and write and look over the yard to the hills and meadows beyond.

Rain tomorrow. It is certain always to rain heavily on the feast of Saints Simon and Jude.

28TH DAY OF OCTOBER, *Feast of Saints Simon and Jude*

Sunny.

29TH DAY OF OCTOBER, *Feast of Saint Colman, an Irish bishop who taught a mouse to keep him awake in chapel*

Aelis has come with a load of puppies from her best hound, a gift from her father to mine, she says. I think she could not wait for my saint's day to see the beautiful George. She heard Mass with us and stayed for dinner and dancing and gossip and supper and now must spend the night as it is too late to ride home. Aelis thought of everything.

I have named the puppies. The little male is Brutus, after the first king of Britain, and the females are all called after herbs: Betony, Rosemary, Anise, and Rue.

30TH DAY OF OCTOBER, *Feast of Saint Marcellus the Centurion, killed for resigning from the army*

I tried after dinner today to get George to play chess with me, but he said he promised the Lady Aelis a walk to acquaint her with our manor. Corpus bones! It is moat and muddy yard, house and stables and barn, dovecote, privy, and pig yard. She could see it all from the hall door.

I watched George and Aelis from my window. When they walk together, she walks straight and slow and quiet. This is not the same Aelis from the high meadow. She looks at George as if he were the king and he looks at her as if she were made of Venetian glass. Seeing them gives me a pain in my liver. I must doctor myself with wormwood and mint.

31ST DAY OF OCTOBER, *Feast of Saint Erc, British martyr, and Allhallows Eve, when ghosts walk*

We sat up late tonight eating nuts and apples, watching the bonfires lit throughout the shire to drive off witches and goblins. Many people are afeared tonight of the dead who come back to visit the earth, but the only dead I know are my tiny brothers and sisters who died before they were born, and how could I be afeared of them? I wish they *would* come visit. It might ease my mother's grieving.

As we roasted apples in the fire, Uncle George told us of the places he has been. I could almost see them as he spoke—the Gravelly Sea, all gravel and sand without a drop of water, which ebbs and flows as other seas do and is full of fishes; the nearby Isle of Giants, home to men thirty feet tall who sleep standing up; and the Isle of Pytar, where the people are tiny as elves and eat nothing, but live by the smell of wild apples. I especially long to see the beasts he described—unicorns, dragons, snails so great men live in their shells, a splendid big beast called an elephant with a tail at each end (this one I think my uncle's fancy), and the incredible whales, fish as big as houses, who could swallow whole a man or a bear or a horse.

My uncle George has brought gaiety and wonder into my life. I will not give him to Aelis and satisfy myself with wormwood cordials!

NOVEMBER ✛

1ST DAY OF NOVEMBER, *which the Saxons call the Month of Blood, Feast of All Saints*

We took down the hazel branches from the doors and windows and blessed God for keeping us free of witches for another year. Would that it were so easy to keep the abominable Robert away. He is coming for Christmas. The first memory I have of this brother is his drowning ants by pissing on the anthill. He has plagued me ever since.

2ND DAY OF NOVEMBER, *Feast of All Souls*

I joined the village children today as they went from cottage to cottage begging for soul cakes. Our cook makes the largest cakes but Perkin's granny makes the best. Ordinarily I do not mind Perkin's granny's muddle-mindedness, for she is the most roomy-hearted person I know, but sometimes she forgets to make her cakes and we all are disappointed.

One year she made cakes at Michaelmas and was full angry that no one came begging for them. Another All Souls Day, as we stood at her window singing, "Soul, a soul, a soul cake, please good mistress, a soul cake," she wished us a Holy Christmas and sang back, "Here we come a-wassailing among the boughs so green." This year she got the day right and I snuck extra cakes into my chamber for tomorrow. I have already eaten them.

3RD DAY OF NOVEMBER, *Feast of Saint Rumwald, who at three days old said "I am a Christian" and died*

The beast my father roared especially ugly roars today. I never seem to please him, although it is true I never try. When I was a child, I ofttimes thought I was a foundling or, even better, the beloved daughter of our good king Edward Longshanks, left here with this beast and his wife for fostering. Mayhap it is true, and now that I near fourteen my real father will call me home. And I will live in a castle with Turkey rugs on the floor and glass in the windows and dress my hair with a comb of gold and ivory. No, even better, my real father is a woodsman from the west who lives in a treehouse made of sticks and branches. He calls me home and we live with the beasts of the forest and dance in the moonlight in the wet grass and no one calls us in to go to bed or finish our sewing, which Morwenna is doing now, the Devil take her.

4TH DAY OF NOVEMBER, *Feast of Saint Birstan, who once when praying for the dead heard them answer "Amen"*

Brought my popinjay to dinner. He fell off my shoulder into the boiled mirling and I had to take him to the kitchen to wash the sauce off his feathers and let him dry himself by the fire. My father roared because there were a few feathers in the fish. He has eaten worse. As I passed his chair after dinner, the beast hit me hard enough to crack my rump.

Afterwards, my uncle George winked at me and made all the uproar worth it. My heart almost stopped.

5TH DAY OF NOVEMBER, *Feast of Saints Zachary and Elizabeth, parents of John the Baptist although they were much too old*

Father Huw came for dinner after Mass. He is infested with boils and blotches and sought the aid of my lady mother. To test my skills in doctoring, she asked what I would advise. I thought the best remedy was to throw himself in the river, but aloud I advised an ointment made of oil of bay and a bath once in a while.

6TH DAY OF NOVEMBER, *Feast of Saint Illtud, who once sailed to Brittany with corn ships to relieve a famine*

Went to the high meadow to meet Aelis as we planned. I waited all day but she never came.

Morwenna caught me sneaking back after supper and I have been made to do extra sewing. My belly is croaking with hunger and I have seven ticks.

7TH DAY OF NOVEMBER, *Feast of Saint Willibrord, archbishop who killed sacred cows, destroyed idols, and still lived to be eighty-one*

Aelis did not come to the meadow yesterday because she was with my uncle George. I have made myself another draft of wormwood and mint.

8TH DAY OF NOVEMBER, *Feast of the Crowned Martyrs, who were either four Roman soldiers or five Persian stonemasons*

I put a toad in George's bed. I don't know why. I cried at dinner and left the table before the almond cream. I don't know why. I looked for Perkin to pinch him but he was gone with the goats. I cannot be a monk nor a crusader nor a tumbler. I must stay here and hem sheets until I die. My humors are greatly out of balance. I prescribe for myself wormwood in spiced wine and some of the custard left from supper. And I will let all of the dogs sleep in my bed.

9TH DAY OF NOVEMBER, *Feast of Saint Theodore the Wonder Worker*

It appears a storm is coming. Father Huw says storms are the work of the Devil. Does that mean if the Devil is busy with some other mischief, the weather is good? Or if the Devil is occupied bringing a storm to Stonebridge, there is no sickness or evil or bad weather elsewhere in the world? Is the Devil then, being in charge of the weather, more powerful than God?

10TH DAY OF NOVEMBER, *Feast of Aed Mac Bricc, bishop and physician of Ireland, who could travel through the air*

Father Huw is ringing the bells to drive the storm away, but the Devil is winning this time.

11TH DAY OF NOVEMBER, *Martinmas, Feast of Saint Martin of Tours, who gave his cloak to a beggar who was Christ in disguise*

The wind ripped the roofs off several of the cottages and the unlucky villagers crowded into our hall last night. Trees fell and the lowlands were flooded with a foot of water as our normally dilly-dally river leapt its banks and ran through the fields, looking for things to devour.

Perkin said babies in their cradles were washed out of the cottages and sailed away to lands unknown like Moses in the Bible. This morning we can see the river tumbling with dead rats, turnip tops, and cooking pots.

12TH DAY OF NOVEMBER, *Feast of Saint Cadwaladr the Battle Shunner*

Why, I wonder, did God make faces with the nose over the mouth instead of the other way? Why do noses have two openings and mouths only one? And why do we need to blow our noses but never our ears? Or our eyes?

I thought to ask Morwenna these questions, but when she doesn't have answers she just bellows at me and sends me to do embroidery, so I dare not risk it. It rains today, so I am sitting in my chamber listening to the music of my birds and wondering.

13TH DAY OF NOVEMBER, *Feast of Saint Abbo of Fleury, killed in a fight between serving men and monks*

My father is confined to his bed with severe ale head. I ground some peony root to soothe his pain but he drank the powder in more ale so I don't know how much good it will do. I wonder why every occasion for mourning or celebrating seems to call for ale: birth ales, church ales, bride ales, funeral ales, harvest ales. Every week our hall is filled with guests who are marking some occasion with ale on one day and violently ridding themselves of it the next. Birds and animals and children, being smarter, never get drunk and never have ale head or putrid stomach.

14TH DAY OF NOVEMBER, *Feast of Saint Dyfrig, the bishop who crowned Arthur king of Britain*

All is ashes. I was in the high meadow today with

Aelis, who says she loves my uncle George, and he loves her, and they wish to wed. I must doubt that her father the baron will let her be given to a younger son with no land and no title, but she says she always gets her way, so I am greatly afeared. Will they, my two most favorite in the world, abandon me for each other? I am sore stricken.

I have heard that if lovers meet a pig while walking, it is certain to doom their love. If only I could arrange for them to meet a pig. Or, even better, a weasel. Where do I get a weasel? And how do I get them all three together? I think to need more wormwood tonight.

15TH DAY OF NOVEMBER, *Feast of Saint Malo, a bishop who sang psalms to his horse*

A gray and drizzly day. I have done extra hours of embroidery, for it gave me time to think undisturbed about Aelis and George. I thought to make a spell to curse them but I do not know where to get dragon dung. Mayhap I should pray instead but I am not very good at asking nicely for things, even from God.

16TH DAY OF NOVEMBER, *Feast of Saint Margaret of Scotland, queen and needleworker*

They are cleaning out the privy today. The stench drove me from the house into the muddy fields, but when they started to spread the manure on the fields, I went back into the house. One thing I will never do is run away and be a privy cleaner.

19TH DAY OF NOVEMBER, *Feast of Saint Hilda, abbess of Whitby, said to be a relative of my mother*

They found the remains of several spindles, many skeins of wool, and an unfinished tapestry in the muck from the privy. Why is everyone so certain they are mine?

18TH DAY OF NOVEMBER, *Feast of Saint Mawes, who can cure headaches, worms, and snakebite*

I have developed a rash on my body where the rough cloth rubs on my skin. I wanted to take a bath, thinking that the dirt on my skin made the rash worse, but the bathing tub has been turned upside down and is being used as an extra table in the kitchen and I cannot have it until spring, so I just spread goose grease on my rash. The dogs are following me everywhere.

19TH DAY OF NOVEMBER, *Feast of Saint Ermenberga, succeeded as abbess by her daughter, Mildred*

Heard Mass three times today. My father must want something of God. A rich son-in-law, no doubt, although there have been no further prune-faced suitors.

No more news of George and Aelis, the uncle thief. Mayhap their love is but a dream of Aelis's. George for certain has said nothing, albeit he has new dark circles about his eyes and no winks for me.

20TH DAY OF NOVEMBER, *Feast of Saint Edmund the King*

It is a strange and wonderful story, about King Edmund. He was hacked to pieces by invading Vikings, and his head rolled under a thorn bush where it lay calling "Help, help" until his friends could find it and carry it home. I have added to the picture on my wall Edmund's head hiding in the bush, calling "Help, help." His teeth are yellow because I have no white paint. But maybe they truly were yellow. Most people's are.

21ST DAY OF NOVEMBER, *Feast of Saint Gelasius, pope, who insisted bishops give one-quarter of their wealth to the poor*

Morwenna says today is the day Noah entered the Ark. I asked her how did she know, was she there? She hates when I make jests about how old she is, so she just sniffed.

22ND DAY OF NOVEMBER, *Feast of Saint Cecilia, who refused to sacrifice to pagan gods and was suffocated in her bathing room*

We were visited by a procession of musicians today celebrating the feast of Cecilia, their special saint. We had music at dinner, with lutes and gitterns and pipes and drums. My favorite song was about Arthur and Guinevere. It was beautifully tragic. I have no talent to be a musician, but I now have it in my mind to be a song maker.

One of the musicians showed me a jest to do with lute strings. He cut one and sprinkled the pieces on a bench near the fire. As they grew hot, they moved and twisted like worms or maggots. One of the dogs was fooled and started barking and scratching at the bench. Then she ate the strings. No one else noticed. A poor jest.

23RD DAY OF NOVEMBER, *Feast of Saint Clement, thrown into the sea with an anchor around his neck*

My mother, Morwenna, and I are spending some days crushing, grinding, boiling, steeping, and straining herbs. The taste and smell of agrimony, betony, feverfew, and dill are in my clothes, my mouth, my hair, my ears. While we worked, my mother told the story of how she first met my father.

She said, "I was the ward of the baron Fulk Longsword, my father having died some years before, and was living at the time with his family in their castle near York. One day appeared a young knight of no great fortune or renown, with great strong arms and shoulders, and eyes like a raven's. He claimed the baron had cheated his father out of a plot of woodland and he, the knight, wanted it back. When the baron laughed and refused, the knight challenged him to a contest on the field of honor.

"The baron bade his men throw the young knight out and we all sat down to supper. I remember we ate minnows and eels baked with white apples. But all night we could hear the knight banging on the gatehouse door with the hilt of his sword, calling out his grievances. It began to rain and then to snow but day after day the knight stayed there, pounding on the door and shouting.

"I was most impressed with his strength and his stubbornness, and so too was the baron, it seems, for he would not let his knights run the young man through with their swords but instead brought him in and listened to him, gave him the woodland, and sat him at his side for dinner. Then the young knight's eyes found me and I knew that strength and stubbornness would win me as they had the baron, whether I would or no, and so I went right upstairs and packed my clothes. In three days we were wed and off to Stonebridge. We were both fifteen."

That was the end of her story. I cannot imagine my father a young knight, but I certainly can see him pounding on the gatehouse door all night. I told my mother then some of my wonderings and about my wanting to be a song maker.

She pulled one of my plaits and said, "Song maker, Birdy? Don't stretch your legs longer than your stockings or your toes will stick out." Then she added, "You are so much already, Little Bird. Why not cease your fearful pounding against the bars of your cage and be content?"

I do not know exactly what that means but it troubles me.

24TH DAY OF NOVEMBER, *Feast of Saint Minver, who threw her comb at the Devil*

Today I asked Morwenna about spells. "What," I asked, "is a spell against warts? Against sickness in sheep? Oh, ah," I asked, feigning innocence, "what would one use for a spell to come between lovers if one has no dragon dung?"

"Facing the lovers by moonlight," she said, "throw dirt from a new-made grave and say 'Love abate. Disintegrate. Turn love to hate,' and what are you up to now, Little Bird?"

That sounds too fearsome to me. I must find a spell that does not involve graves.

25TH DAY OF NOVEMBER, *Feast of Saint Catherine, a virgin of Alexandria whose body was broken on a spiked wheel*

Catherine, who is my own name saint, was, I know, a princess who refused to marry a pagan emperor, but I do not understand the part about her dying on a spiked wheel. What is a spiked wheel? Where are the spikes? What is it for, besides martyring virgins? How was she fastened on? Was it lying on the ground or upright? Why didn't they just put an arrow through her?

Would I choose to die rather than be forced to marry? I hope to avoid the issue, for I do not think I have it in me to be a saint.

Inspired by the musicians, I made a Saint Catherine song. It begins:

Catherine, bless your namesake today.
If I ever meet a pagan king, to you
    I'll pray.
Hi diddly, hey diddly, sing ho.

For save yourself you didn't know how
But being a saint mayhap could do
    better now.
Hi diddly, hey diddly, sing ho.

This is as far as I have gotten. The hi diddlys are my favorite part.

26TH DAY OF NOVEMBER, *Feast of Saint Marcellus, a prince seized by heretics and hurled to his death from a high rock*

I am confined to my chamber with my embroidery needle. My mother's doing. How it came about is this. Yesterday being my saint's day and my birthday, there was a feast. We sat down to dinner at an hour before noon and stayed at table until after dark. The hall was crowded with guests, musicians, and servers and was—for once—overwarm. We ate glazed eggs, apple tarts, whole pigeons and snipes, peacock in raisin sauce, red and white jellies, pig stomach stuffed with eggs and spices, and potted beef with nutmeg. I relished it all but the birds, which I never eat. During the feast, the cook and the kitchen boys paraded around the hall with a giant pastry they had made to honor me of Saint Catherine dying on her wheel, with marzipan spikes and spun sugar soldiers. The wheel was upright.

The eating went on forever. I was seated next my father, so I had no one to talk with. George was not there, so I had no one to look at. Finally I conceived a small amusement to pass the time. I took a string from the lute that once was mine but now belongs to the cook, cut it into pieces as the traveling musician had showed me, and sprinkled them on a dish of creamed herring as it passed by.

The heat of the dish made the pieces of string writhe and wiggle. The lady Margaret, seated three places beyond me, dipped her hand ladylike into the dish and lifted a piece of fish to her mouth. Screeching like a barn owl, she jumped up and set about wiping her hand on her gown, the tablecloth, my father, whatever she could reach. The cook was summoned. I thought I was safe and he would be blamed but somehow it was sorted out and my saint's day ended with the cook standing on the table, shaking his spoon at me and swearing in Saxon. I was sent from the table to prepare a potion of cinnamon and milk for the daughter of the lord of Moreton Manor, who fainted in the potted meat. What a ninny. Now I am imprisoned. Deus! It was meant as a jest.

27TH DAY OF NOVEMBER, *Feast of Saint Fergus, an Irish bishop, who condemned irregular marriages, sorcerers, and priests who wear their hair long*

I am still confined to my chamber, with the army of girls here for my saint's day celebrations. Aelis, the uncle thief, is with us and I do not know how to act toward her. I have chosen for now slightly cold but well behaved.

Aelis says her father will not speak to her of marriage to my uncle, and George has not said one word to her this entire visit. For one who claims to be perishing of love, she looks healthy enough.

Perkin's granny says to put yarrow up their noses and spit, and Aelis and George will love no more. Corpus bones! I could more easily get dirt from a hundred graves than stuff yarrow up George's nose!

28TH DAY OF NOVEMBER, *Feast of Saint Juthwara, who wore cheeses on her chest and was beheaded by her stepbrother*

As Aelis and I passed George on the way in to supper, I threw a fistful of dirt at each of them, spattering us all. It was not really from a grave, but from the edge of the churchyard, yet it must suffice, for I am not venturing deep into any graveyard with this jealous evil in my heart. George and Aelis looked dusty, puzzled, and sore vexed.

I said the turn-love-to-hate chant under my breath so no one could hear me, for sure else I would be punished, cast away, locked up, or laughed at, no one of which I relish. I do not know how long it will take the spell to work. By supper's end they did not yet look like people whose love had turned to hate.

29TH DAY OF NOVEMBER, *Feast of Saints Paramon and others, three hundred seventy-five martyrs killed in a single day*

After supper yestereve George accompanied the baron's party back to Finbury Castle. George is now home again, ill-tempered and drunk. Corpus bones, all that men seem to know of doctoring is prescribing ale.

When will the curse work?

30TH DAY OF NOVEMBER, *Feast of Saint Andrew, fisherman, apostle, and martyr, missionary to Greece, Turkey, and Poland*

Three weeks and three days before Christmas comes in. I had it in my mind to make a Christmas song, but I can think of nothing to say except when will the curse work?

**D**ECEMBER ✤

2ND DAY OF DECEMBER, *Feast of Saint Bibiana, beaten with leaden whips until she died*

So troubled was I by events of yesterday that I did not write but sat long with my mother, who sang and stroked my hair as if I were a child. This is how it happened.

The sun looked likely to shine yestermorn, so Gerd the miller's son and I left our chores undone and went to Wooton village where they were to hang two thieves. Never having seen a hanging, I could only imagine the huge hairy bandits with cruel scarred faces, snarling and growling fearsome curses, while we onlookers shrieked and shrank back in fear. I thought it sounded better even than a feast or a fair. Perkin could not be found, so I made the clay-brained Gerd go with me.

It looked to be a gay occasion, even though the

rain started before we were far along, which dampened our spirits a little and our shoes a lot. The sheriff had just constructed a new gallows, so the whole village turned out to celebrate. People were packed all around the church square, villagers and strangers, priests and children, peddlers and players, and hawkers selling every kind of food and drink. I bought sausages, bread, an onion, two meat pies, and an apple pastry and ate most of it, for it was my penny, not Gerd's.

We were all laughing and shouting when we saw the sheriff pull the cart in. I was calling "Dead bandits never rob again," which I thought quite clever, as the cart passed me by, carrying the two bandits, ropes already tied about their necks.

The sheriff dragged them from the cart and up the ladder to the gallows. Corpus bones! They were no more than twelve years old, skinny, frightened, and dirty. Their scared stupid faces knocked the jolly right out of me, and when one leaned off the platform and grabbed my sleeve, slobbering and crying "Help me, noble lady!" I turned and ran. I was near out of the village before the first was shoved off the platform, but I could hear the cheering and laughing behind me.

Gerd caught up with me and we left Wooton, the clodpole rubbing his eyes with his grubby fists in sadness for missing the fun. I vomited up my bread and sausage but Gerd kept his. All the way back to the Stonebridge road, we could hear the laughing and cheering of the crowd.

The wretched day grew worse still, for on our way home we saw a funeral procession ride down the road toward London. It was midday and the rain had slowed to a drizzle, but it was near as dark as dusk. Never have I seen so many men and horses so quiet, their bells and bridles muffled. The only sound was the thud of the horses' hooves on the wet ground.

First came a crowd of men wrapped in black cloaks. I could not tell who they were but the tall man in front had the saddest face I ever saw. Following them, two horses—one before and one after—carried a sort of litter with the coffin. And in the rear marched hundreds of soldiers in battle dress, without a smile or a wave for us, without a sound, except for the slow measured tread of their boots.

Gerd and I ran home, trembling with fear that the king had died, for who else would be taken to London with such a company, such pomp, and such grief? The king had been king as long as I had lived. How could we have another? What would happen to us? Gerd went to the mill and I burst into the hall as if the Devil were pulling my hair. My mother was there, getting spices for the cook from the locked cupboard, and I ran to her, crying for the king and myself.

"No, Little Bird," she said, "you weep for the wrong person. It is not the king who is dead, but Eleanor, his kind and gentle queen."

On her way to join the king as he warred against the Scots, the queen took ill and died. The king, broken of heart, came from Scotland to take her back to London. He built a towering stone cross to mark the place where she lay at Lincoln Castle and will have one built at every stop from here to London. I knew then who the tall sad-faced man was. I had seen the king, finally, for the first time, and there was no cheering or celebrating or glee, only grief. I had cried with the king.

I told my mother then about the little bandits and losing my sausage and seeing the sad procession, and she cooed and comforted me and forgot to scold me for running off. This made me feel some better, but what comforted me the most was the thought of telling it all to Perkin.

Morwenna says that fairies have the faces of beloved dead and that some people who have seen fairies recognize their faces. I think I would not be afeared to meet a fairy with the queen's face, God save her.

3RD DAY OF DECEMBER, *Feast of Saint Birinus, apostle of Wessex, first bishop of Dorchester, and builder of churches*

George was drunk again all day. Aelis has been taken to London for the king's Christmas court. He never says her name. Is it the curse?

4TH DAY OF DECEMBER, *Feast of Saint Barbara, said to have been martyred in Nicomedia, Heliopolis, Tuscany, and Rome*

My brother Thomas has come from serving the king to spend Christmas with us. Because of the rain he arrived so sodden and beslombered with muck that I did not know him. He is near a stranger to me, as he is much with the king, but does not seem as abominable as Robert, so I shall not overly vex him.

Thomas says the king, still on his way to London with the queen, does not weep but rides with a face of stone, so deeply does he grieve. I wonder if the mothers of the two boy bandits hanged at Wooton grieve for them. I find I prefer fairs and feasts to hangings.

5TH DAY OF DECEMBER, *Feast of Saint Crispina, who was shaved bald to humiliate her before she was beheaded*
Thomas, very lordly in his patterned hose and pointed shoes, played the child long enough to coach the village boys in their fighting games. As I sat in the sun with my eyes closed, I could hear the thud of wooden swords on wooden shields, the screams of the dying and joyous shouts of the victors, the furious whinnying of those boys doomed to be horses instead of knights, and I pretended I was on crusade. I shall not tell George this.

6TH DAY OF DECEMBER, *Feast of Saint Nicholas, who loves children, pawnbrokers, and sailors*
There are no Jews left in England today, Thomas says. By order of the king they have all left the country. I find it hard to believe that the old lady and the

little soft-eyed girl who stayed in our hall could be a danger to England. Is it blasphemy to ask God to protect Jews? I will ask Edward.

Or maybe not. Mayhap I will whisper it just to God and trust it is all right. God keep the Jews.

7TH DAY OF DECEMBER, *Feast of Saint Ambrose, proclaimed bishop of Milan before he was even a Christian*

Thomas says the king and the people of his court have chosen each his own special profanity so that they don't have to say "Deus!" or "Corpus bones!" or "Benedicite!" as we ordinary folk do. The king says "God's breath!" His son says "God's teeth!" Thomas says "God's feet!" I, not being ordinary, shall choose one also. I will try one on each day and see what fits me best. Today it is: God's face!

8TH DAY OF DECEMBER, *Feast of Saint Budoc who was born at sea in a barrel*

God's ears, it is cold! The sun shines on a fairy world carved from ice. No one stirs outside. I think all of creation is huddled in our hall, so I have sneaked into my chamber. The fireplace is not lit, but I can pull the feather bed up to my chin and write in peace, even though the candle flame spits and sputters in the wind and I have twice overturned the ink.

The magpie's water was frozen over this morning, so I have covered all the cages with kirtles and gowns and mantles to keep my birds warm. Mayhap they will think it night until God warms the world again.

9TH DAY OF DECEMBER, *Feast of Saint Wolfeius, first hermit in Norfolk*

God's knees! A person can only wear one gown and one kirtle at a time, so why are my mother and her ladies making such a fuss about my covering the bird cages with their spare ones! I cannot believe they would want my poor birds to freeze to death.

I will have plenty of time to think on this, for I am imprisoned in the solar, brushing feathers and seed and bird dung off of what seems enough clothing for the French army. I see no deliverance. Perkin is busy with his grandmother. Aelis is in London with the king. George and Thomas are from home much these days, riding and drinking and amusing other people and not me. God's knees, I might as well be an orphan.

10TH DAY OF DECEMBER, *Feast of Saint Eulalia, virgin and martyr, who spat at her judge and was burned alive*

God's nails, Morwenna is in a sour temper today. Every time I open my mouth, she cracks my knuckles with her spindle.

11TH DAY OF DECEMBER, *Feast of Saint Daniel, who lived thirty-three years atop a pillar*

Morwenna threatens to truss me like a goose and dump me in the river if I continue in my quest for the perfect profanity. God's chin! She treats me like a child.

12TH DAY OF DECEMBER, *Feast of Saints Mercuria, Dionysia, Ammonaria, and the other Ammonaria, holy women killed by heathens*

I have chosen. God's thumbs! What a time I have had in deciding. I chose God's thumbs because thumbs are such important things and handy to use. I thought to make a list of all the things I could not do without my thumbs, like writing, plaiting my hair, and pulling Perkin by his ear, but now it seems to me to be a waste of paper and ink, for I can think of no purpose for such a list unless some heathen Turk came from across the sea and threatened to cut off my thumbs with his golden sword and I was able to convince him to spare my thumbs by reading him my list of how important thumbs are, but since it seems unlikely both that a Turk would threaten my thumbs and that a list would stop him if he did, I shall save the time and the ink and not make a list.

13TH DAY OF DECEMBER, *Feast of Saint Judoc, whose hair and beard grew after his death and had to be trimmed by his followers*

Storm again today. George and Thomas are still gone, but we are cooped up in here like chickens in a hen house. I stayed out of Morwenna's sight so she would not set me to some lady-task. I used the time to wonder and have made a wondering song:

Why aren't fingers equal lengths?
What makes cold?
Why do men get old and bald
And women only old?
When does night turn into day?
How deep is the sea?
How can rivers run uphill?
What will become of me?

14TH DAY OF DECEMBER, *Feast of Saint Hybald, abbot of our own Lincolnshire. I wonder if he is a relative*

I am in disgrace today. Grown quite weary with my embroidery, with my pricked fingers and tired eyes and sore back, I kicked it down the stairs to the hall, where the dogs fought and slobbered over it, so I took the soggy mess and threw it to the pigs.

Morwenna grabbed me by the ear and pinched my face. My mother gave me a gentle but stern lecture about behaving like a lady. Ladies, it seems, seldom have strong feelings and, if they do, never never let them show. God's thumbs! I always have strong feelings and they are quite painful until I let them out, like a cow who needs to give milk and bellows with the pain in her teats. So I am in disgrace in my chamber. I pray Morwenna never discovers that being enchambered is no punishment for me. She would find some new torture, like sending me to listen to the ladies in the solar.

15TH DAY OF DECEMBER, *Feast of Saint Offa, king of*

*the East Saxons, who left his wife, his lands, his family,
and his country to become a monk in Rome and die*

I was seated at dinner this day with a visitor from
Kent, another clodpole in search of a wife. This one
was friendly and good-tempered, and had all his
teeth and hair. But he did not compare with George
or Perkin, so I would have none of him. Our talk at
dinner went like this:

"Do you enjoy riding, Lady Catherine?"

"Mmph."

"Could we perhaps ride together while I am here?"

"Pfgh."

"I understand you read Latin. I admire learned
women when they are also beautiful."

"Urgh."

"Mayhap you could show me about the manor after
dinner."

"Grmph."

So it went until I conceived my plan, after realizing
that the only thing my father would want more than a
rich son-in-law is not to part with one of his pennies or
acres or bushels of onions. So I grew quite lively and
talkative, bubbling with praise for our chests of treasure and untold acres and countless tenants and hoards
of silver and for the modesty that prompted my father
to hide his wealth and appear as a mere country
knight. My suitor's eyes, which had already rested
kindly on me, caught fire, and he fairly flew over the
rushes to talk with my father in the solar.

The storm I expected was not long in coming.

Poor Fire Eyes tumbled down the stairs from the solar, hands over his head, and rolled across the hall floor to the door and out while my father bellowed from above, "Dowry! Manors! Treasure! You want me to pay you to take the girl? Dowry? I'll give you her dowry!"

And as the comely young man ran across the yard on his way to the stable and freedom, a brimming chamber pot came flying from the solar window and landed on his head. Farewell, suitor. Benedicite.

Even now as I pity the young man in his spoiled tunic, I must smile to think of my dowry. No other maiden in England has one like it.

16TH DAY OF DECEMBER, *Feast of Saint Bean, lakeside hermit of Ireland*

My breath stinks, my gut grumbles, and my liver is oppilated. It must be all this fish. Would that Christmas come soon and bring an end to fasting. I am turning into a herring.

AFTER VESPERS, LATER THIS DAY: My uncle George is leaving Stonebridge. He does not eat but only drinks his meals. His cheeks are dusky with unshaved whiskers. He has no stories or winks or grins for me anymore. Is it the curse? Do I have powers?

17TH DAY OF DECEMBER, *Feast of Saint Lazarus, who was raised from the dead by Jesus and later went to France*

George has gone to York. He did not say goodbye, so I do not know if he will be back for Christmas. I do not know if the curse worked. I will miss him but I liked him better before he loved Aelis. I think love is like mildew, growing gray and musty on things, spoiling them, and smelling bad.

18TH DAY OF DECEMBER, *Feast of Saint Mawnan, an Irish bishop who kept a pet ram*

The cold has trapped us inside again and I am grown full restless. This is how I have spent my day: I was awakened at dawn by Wat dropping the wood as he lit my fire. I put on my undertunic and stockings while still under the covers for warmth and then, breaking the ice in the bowl, splashed water on my face and hands. I dressed in my yellow gown with the blue kirtle over, my red shoes, and my cloak, even though I was not going outside. Morwenna helped me plait my hair, which we trimmed with silver pins.

We could not hear Mass for we could not get through the snow to the church, so I breakfasted with bread and ale. The next two hours I hemmed sheets in the solar while I listened to my mother's ladies chatter about the Christmas feast. We ate dinner very quickly, for the snow falling through the smokehole in the hall kept dousing the fire. I then hurried back to the solar where it was noisy but warm, and here I am now, writing and wishing I were outside on the meadow and Perkin was playing the pipes and the goats were nuzzling one another and me. It is many hours until supper and bed.

19TH DAY OF DECEMBER, *Feast of Saint Nemesius, acquitted of theft but executed for being a Christian*

The little book of saints never disappoints me. I have kept it with me since the abbot sent it. I showed it once to my mother, who exclaimed over the pictures, listened to a story or two, and then forgot about it. I therefore consider it mine. Or almost mine. Or near enough, for here it is in my chamber.

20TH DAY OF DECEMBER, *Feast of Saints Ammon, Zeno, Ptolemy, Ingenes, and Theophilus, soldiers martyred by the Romans*

Too dull for writing.

21ST DAY OF DECEMBER, *Feast of Saint Thomas the Apostle, the shortest day and longest night of the year*

The snow has stopped. Life begins again.

Last night I tucked a pin into an onion and put it under my pillow so I would dream of my future husband. I dreamed only of onions and in the morning had to wash my hair. It near froze before it dried.

We feasted this day in honor of my brother Thomas, whose saint's day this is. We had oceans of fish and acres of dried apples, and musicians and jugglers and tumblers, and so many guests there were no benches for the young men, who had to sit on the soiled rushes and grab at food as best they could. I am still dazzled by the acrobats and the magician who carried fire in a linen napkin and pulled roses from my ear!

22ND DAY OF DECEMBER, *Feast of Saints Chaeremon, Ischyrion, and other Egyptian Christians, who were driven into the desert and never seen again*

My chamber is full of visiting girls here to celebrate Christmas. They twitter and chatter louder than my birds, but it does not sound like music to me. I cannot think so I cannot write. No more to say. I miss Aelis. I worry for George. Did the curse work?

23RD DAY OF DECEMBER, *Feast of Saint Victoria, a Roman virgin stabbed to death for refusing to sacrifice to idols*

The abominable Robert has arrived for the Christmas feast. He brought no gifts, as did my uncle George, and no tales of court, as did Thomas, but only his gross yellow-toothed self. He sows turmoil everywhere. Pinched me where I sit and threatened to roast my birds for Christmas dinner. Made one of the maids cry. Set the dogs to fighting until my father threw them out into the snow. Teased Thomas about his obvious passion for the daughter of Arnulf of Weddingford. Robert told him that every man needs a horse, a sword, and a woman, but he should love only the first two.

24TH DAY OF DECEMBER, *Eve of Christmas Day and*

Feast of Saint Mochua of Timahoe, an Irish monk who was once a soldier

Another bright clear day so we were able to search the woods for mistletoe, holly, and ivy to hang in the hall. Thomas and his friend Ralph acted out the battle of the holly and ivy, arguing over who God loved best, bickering in high voices and shamming a tournament of plants. We all laughed and cheered them. It was a treat to be without Robert, who now that he is twenty thinks our games childish and beneath him.

As I write this, I can see from the open window the parade of villagers leading a cow, an ox, and an ass to the manger in the church. Soon fires will be lit upon the hills, Wat will bring in the yule log, and Christmas will begin.

25TH DAY OF DECEMBER, *Christmas Day*

Waes hail! The hall was overstuffed today for the Christmas feast, with villagers and guests and Thomas's friends from court. Even my nip-cheese father forebore to complain about the cost, today being Christmas Day. We ate, of course, boar's head, which the cook's assistant carried about the hall on a platter decorated with apples and ivy. We also had herring pie, fried milk, onion and mustard omelette, turnip soup, figs stuffed with cinnamon and hard-boiled eggs, mulled pear cider, and more.

We had hardly finished eating when we heard "Please to let the mummers in," and the Christmas play began. Perkin was a wise man, of course. Thomas Baker was Joseph, and Gerd the miller's son played the evil King Herod, although, like Gerd, Herod seemed more stupid than evil. Elfa the laundress was the Virgin Mary; it was to be Beryl, John At-Wood's daughter, but since Michaelmas she is breeding and no virgin in real life or in mumming.

I was very stirred when John Over-Bridge carried in the gilt star on a long pole, which the three wise men and the shepherds followed to the Holy Manger. The villagers who played the shepherds thought to make the play more lively by leading real sheep to the cradle where the Christ Child lay. One began to eat the rushes off the floor and two others, frighted by the dogs, ran off, knocking into each other, the shepherds, the other players, the table, the torches. We all joined in a great chase about the hall after the bawling and kicking sheep. Finally Perkin used his best goatherd voice to calm the sheep and lead them outside, and the play finished with just two wise men. The shepherds were right. It was much more lively.

After the play we played Snapdragons. William Steward burned his hand trying to snatch a raisin from the flaming pan. I anointed it with a paste of sow bugs, moss, and goose grease, although he said he suffered more from the stink than from the pain of the burn. My mother then bade us play a game where no one gets burned, so we changed to Hot Cockles, where people only get smacked.

The hall is full of sleeping bodies tonight. I had to step carefully over those on the floor so I could snatch more figs from the kitchen. If there is sticky on these pages, it is from figs. I love them well.

26TH DAY OF DECEMBER, *Feast of Saint Stephen, stoned to death for blasphemy. First day of Christmas*

Perkin was chosen the Lord of Misrule, so he is Master of the Christmas Revels and we must obey him until Christmas is over. We made him a scepter wound with holly and a crown of pig bones, ivy, and bay and are hilariously following his orders. Even my father laughed at Perkin's fantastic fooling.

He knighted the dogs and led them on crusade against the barn cats. He made me fetch him ale and pinched me for all the times I've pinched him. He sat Morwenna on his lap and ordered my mother to bring them hot wine. Then he set us to making riddles, promising a reward for the best. I won for my riddle: What is the bravest thing in the world? The neckband of my brother Robert's cloak, for each day it clasps a beast by the throat. I was quite proud until I learned the reward was a kiss from Perkin, so I pouted and left. Robert pinched me as I passed him.

27TH DAY OF DECEMBER, *Saint John's Day. Second day of Christmas*

Thomas, his friend Ralph, my father, two kitchen boys, and Gerd the miller's son all came to me seeking a cure for excessive wassailing. I doctored them with a tonic made of anise and betony and advised them to drink less and vomit more.

28TH DAY OF DECEMBER, *Childermas, the Feast of the Holy Babes and Sucklings, killed by King Herod. Third day of Christmas*

Morwenna says today is the unluckiest day of the year. She made me stay inside my chamber and won't let me sew or embroider for fear I will prick myself, so for me it is not so unlucky.

It is also Perkin's birthday and I think he is not unlucky. He never sews or weaves or goes to bed when someone else says. On summer nights he sleeps outside with the goats, who love him but never tell him what to do. I think Perkin is the luckiest person I know.

29TH DAY OF DECEMBER, *Saint Thomas of Canterbury's Day. Fourth day of Christmas*

Our Lord Perkin declared a tournament for us and the chickens. Although the chickens had silver gilt helmets and twig swords, we won. Chicken for dinner.

30TH DAY OF DECEMBER, *Feast of Saint Egwin, bishop of Worcester. Fifth day of Christmas*

More laughter and singing and arguing and shouting and noise tonight. I have come to my chamber to escape the constant chattering, although even here I am not alone. I am crowded by the visiting girls and their words, words, words.

31ST DAY OF DECEMBER, *Feast of Saint Sylvester, the pope who cured the emperor Constantine of leprosy. Sixth day of Christmas*

It is not snowing today, so I took my mare Blanchefleur for a ride through the frozen fields. I felt great need of solitude and quiet. The manor is so crowded that the privy is the only place I can be alone, and it is too cold to stay there for long. Besides, with so many guests it is the busiest place on the manor.

I brought Blanchefleur back to the barn before supper and stumbled over Robert and Elfa the laundress snuggled into the hay. It appears they will have to get another Virgin Mary for the Christmas play next year.

January

1ST DAY OF JANUARY, *Feast of the Circumcision of Our Lord. Seventh day of Christmas*

Perkin wants me to teach him to read. He dreams of being a scholar but most likely will just be a goat boy who can read. My Latin is none so good—I wish Edward were here to help. But Edward is not here, and Robert and Thomas cannot read or write. Robert can barely talk. Too bad Perkin doesn't want to learn how to skewer an enemy on a sword or tumble a laundress in the barn.

2ND DAY OF JANUARY, *Feast of Saint Abel the Patriarch, son of Adam killed by his brother Cain. Eighth day of Christmas*

New snow today. We had a snowball fight and everyone joined in. Even my lady mother was giddy and gay, laughing and blushing and acting much like a girl although she must be over thirty. William Steward grew smitten and made flowery speeches to her, but we put snow down his pants to cool his passion.

3RD DAY OF JANUARY, *Feast of Saint Genevieve, who through fasting and praying kept Attila the Hun from Paris. Ninth day of Christmas*

My head aches from the cold, the smoke, and the noise of too many people drinking too much ale. At supper, grown angry with the puppies nipping at my food, I swept them off the table onto the floor. Later in remorse I smuggled them all into my bed for the night. Good thing Morwenna sleeps heavy and never knows what she has been sleeping with until morning.

4TH DAY OF JANUARY, *Feast of Saints Aquilinus, Geminus, Eugenius, Marcianus, Quinctus, Theodotus, and Tryphon, a band of martyrs put to death in Africa by the king of the Vandals. Tenth day of Christmas*

The eels in their tub in the kitchen froze last night, so we had an eel feast for dinner and eel pie for supper. I fear more eels with our breakfast bread and ale tomorrow.

5TH DAY OF JANUARY, *Feast of Saint Simeon Stylites, who lived for thirty-seven years atop a pillar, praising God. Eleventh day of Christmas*

I will not be sorry to see the Christmas days end,

for I have been spending excessive time curing other people's ale head, putrid stomach, and various wounds, cuts, and bruises sustained in drunken fights. I have near run out of mustard seed and boiled snake.

6TH DAY OF JANUARY, *Feast of the Epiphany. Twelfth day of Christmas*

The end of Christmas. Mayhap I will soon have my chamber and my bed to share with only the usual residents.

At dinner today my mother found the bean in her Twelfth Cake and chose my father to be king. I found the pea and was queen. My father and I had to sit next each other for the mumming and lead the dancing and eat together at supper. I could hardly swallow from being so near the beast for so long. I wish I had just eaten the pea and told no one.

The best part of the day was when the mummers came in all wigged and masked, donkeys and kings and giants, singing and stomping and clashing their wooden swords. They hardly looked like the villagers I know, although I recognized Sym by his enormous feet and John At-Wood by his red hair, which poked right through his Father Christmas wig.

Spoke John: "In come I, Old Father Christmas, welcome or welcome not. I hope Old Father Christmas will never be forgot."

And the play began, with knights and dragons and battles and the wondrous rebirth of Saint George.

Perkin was Saint George—"Here come I, Saint George. I am called Saint George for Saint George is my name"—and he looked golden and beautiful like a saint and not much like a goat boy, even when his golden wig fell off and Brutus ate it. The dragon he battled was fearsome and bellowed so convincingly that I forgot it was but paper and wood and gears from the mill: "I am the iron dragon which no sword can undo. I eat the small, the pure, the young, and spit their bones at you!" It was gruesome and ugly and will give me nightmares. Perfect.

7TH DAY OF JANUARY, *Feast of Saint Lucian of Antioch, leader of the Lucianists*

I had not a nightmare last night but a dream. Again my uncle George came to rescue me from a dragon. The dragon threw at George a handful of dirt, which turned into a bolt of lightning, and George died at my feet. Has the curse then worked? Is George in danger? What does it mean?

8TH DAY OF JANUARY, *Plough Monday and Feast of Saint Nathalan, farmer*

Today the villagers celebrated what would have been the first day of work since before Christmas if they weren't celebrating instead. I walked down to the churchyard and watched the village boys dancing and fooling. I wonder which is the day when ladies dance and fool.

9TH DAY OF JANUARY *Feast of Saint Fillan, ancient Irish abbot, whose bell and staff and arm still survive*

Now that Christmas is over, we are putting the manor to rights again. Morwenna made me help the kitchen boys dig out the pits and bones and dog droppings from the rushes on the hall floor. We found a silver gilt belt with jeweled buckle, three shoes, a lady's stocking, a wad of fake hair, a rat skeleton, and two silver pennies. I also found Ralf Emory's knife that he accused Walter of Pennington of stealing. Walter is going to the king to complain and there may be a joust between them at the next tournament, though no one stole it after all—it fell into the rushes. Should I tell? I would dearly love to see that joust.

This afternoon we sprinkled dried mint and thyme and gillyflowers over the cleaned rushes. The hall smells much better, but that may be because Robert is not here today.

10TH DAY OF JANUARY, *Feast of Saint Paul of Thebes, the first hermit. He lived to be one hundred thirteen and two lions dug his grave*

A very special holiday—Robert has left. He took with him Brutus, my favorite of the pups, even though I cried and argued and thumped him on the chest with my fists. As they were riding out the gate, Brutus made water in Robert's lap and now I have him back. I think the little creature is bruised and frightened so he will sleep in my bed tonight. Morwenna and the Eternal Guests will just have to make room. Thomas leaves tomorrow. I will be sorry to see him go.

11TH DAY OF JANUARY *Feast of Saint Hyginus, pope and martyr*

The ice on the river has finally frozen hard enough to walk on. Perkin and Gerd the miller's son came to the kitchen for bones that they will polish and fasten to their shoes so they can glide on the ice. I begged my mother to be allowed to go, but she had a headache and would not speak of it. I made her a potion of peony root and oil of roses to soothe her head. Being angry, I wanted to add spurge and deadly hemlock to it, but mostly I love her, so I didn't. Instead I thought to make a list of all the things girls are not allowed to do:

go on crusade
be horse trainers
be monks
laugh very loud
wear breeches
drink in ale houses
cut their hair
piss in the fire to make it hiss
wear nothing
be alone

get sunburned

run

marry whom they will

glide on the ice

12TH DAY OF JANUARY, *Feast of Saint Benedict Biscop, who collected books*

I have heard that a cloth merchant in Lincoln has a privy not in the yard but inside his house, in a little room built out over a stream so that the stream washes the waste away. Such a wonder! I have it in my mind to go to Lincoln and see for myself. I would sit in the privy and piss and think about my water flying through the air, sailing on the stream to the river to the sea and across to wondrous foreign lands. If I cannot go to faraway places, I would like to think my water went.

13TH DAY OF JANUARY, *Feast of Saint Kentigern, called Mungo, grandson of a British prince*

It appears the curse has worked. George returned last night from York to say that Aelis has been married to the seven-year-old duke of Warrington. After the ceremony, the duke had an attack of putrid throat and had to go home to his mother to be nursed. His new wife remains at court.

I am sorry that Aelis was sold at auction to the highest bidder like a horse at a horse fair, but I am gladdened to have my uncle George back.

14TH DAY OF JANUARY, *Feast of Saint Felix of Nola, tortured but not martyred*

I tried to talk to George. He will not hear Aelis's name. He will not speak it. He does not listen, will not play, and his eyes that once flashed mischief and joy now glow dark with pain.

I thought to write a song about his doomed romance, but he said to save it for his betrothal to Ethelfritha, the very rich widow of a salt merchant from York. I asked him if he loved her. He said he loved her money, her business, and her good heart, and that was enough.

I think my curse was cursed. Aelis is gone from here, wedded to a baby. George sighs and suffers. And still he is not mine but marries some fat Saxon widow. God's thumbs. I might have done better to fail. My guts are grumbling. I hope it is but a cold in my liver, but I fear it is guilt and remorse.

15TH DAY OF JANUARY, *Feast of Saint Ita, foster mother of the Irish saints*

George has left for York again. My guts still grumble.

16TH DAY OF JANUARY, *Feast of Saint Henry, who became a hermit rather than marry*

It is none so bad sometimes to have a pig for a father. This day it served me well. There were guests at dinner but I had no forewarning of danger so I acted like myself, some good and some bad, like always. I told the story of the time Perkin and I dressed his smelliest goat in his granny's other shift and let it loose in the church while a visiting friar was preaching about the terrors of Hell. The villagers in the church, convinced that the preacher had loosed the Devil on them, stumbled over each other trying to escape the fiend. Perkin's granny recognized her shift and started chasing the goat to get it back, swinging at him with a candlestick. The frightened goat loosed its bowels in the middle of the church, bawled frantically, and leapt into Perkin's lap. It was wondrous sport, but the story did not seem to amuse my listeners at dinner. We finished eating in quiet.

Later I discovered that one of the guests was another suitor, who was pleased with me and even my story but so offended by my father's burping and farting and scratching his chest with his knife that any hopes for a marriage died. I shall never tell my father that I am grateful to him.

17TH DAY OF JANUARY, *Feast of Saint Antony of Egypt, gardener and mat maker*

A freeze. My ink froze and I had to thaw it over the fire so I could write. But now I have nothing to say.

18TH DAY OF JANUARY, *Feast of Saint Ulfrid, martyred for breaking up a statue of Thor with his axe*

In the heart of winter when we eat for weeks on end porridge and beans, eggs and wrinkled apples, salted meat and dried herring, I think I will never again see peaches and plums, fresh fish and parsley and leeks. I have painted into the mural on my chamber wall a tree bursting with fresh fruit, dripping its juice straight into the waiting mouth of a golden warrior mounted on a black stallion, with my face (the warrior, not the horse).

19TH DAY OF JANUARY *Feast of Saints Marius, Martha, Audifax, and Abachum, a family of Persians martyred while on pilgrimage to Rome*

Much activity about the manor as lambing started at the same time as a snowstorm. The sheep have all been driven to the pen in our yard, and the pregnant ewes will be put in our barn. Many are dropping their lambs on the way, and the shepherds with the newborn lambs stuck in their shirts look like fat bishops.

20TH DAY OF JANUARY, *Feast of Saint Sebastian, who was shot with arrows, recovered, accused the emperor of cruelty, and then was clubbed to death*

Edgar, the saddler's apprentice, is missing. He went outside to relieve his bladder in the middle of the night and never returned. William Steward and the villagers searched for him today but it has been snowing so hard since last morning that they have little hope of finding him.

21ST DAY OF JANUARY *Saint Agnes's Day*

Another virgin martyred rather than marry a heathen. I wonder what is so bad about heathens. They couldn't be worse than Robert.

22ND DAY OF JANUARY, *Feast of Saint Vincent of Saragossa, imprisoned, starved, racked, and roasted*

I crept out last night hoping to help with the lambing. I am none too fond of sheep, for they are stupid and smelly and bad-tempered, but the new lambs are so sweet and soft. No one noticed me, so I sat wrapped in my cloak with lambs asleep in my lap and made a lambing song, which I misremember now, but I know it was good.

23RD DAY OF JANUARY, *Feast of Saint Emerentiana, foster sister of Saint Agnes, stoned to death while praying at her tomb*

Edgar was found. He lost his way back to his cottage in the storm and took shelter in an old shed, which was soon covered in drifting snow. By morning the snow was too heavy for him to shift, so he stayed trapped under it these four days. This morning one of the shepherds spied a stick that Edgar managed to force through the snow with a stocking tied on and he was dug out. Thanks to God, he had not really gone to the privy but was sneaking back to his cottage from our hen house with his shirt stuffed with eggs, so he had plenty to eat.

24TH DAY OF JANUARY, *Feast of Saint Timothy, who was clubbed to death during the pagan festival of Katagogia*

The only Latin we have for Perkin to learn to read from is documents and house accounts, so I made some simple stories in my best Latin and am teaching Perkin from them. He says he is certain a scholar has to be able to read more than *Pater meus animalus est* or *Non amo Robertum*. I am doing my best.

26TH DAY OF JANUARY, *Feast of Saint Paula, a Roman widow who became a Christian, renounced all amusements, and went to visit the hermits in the Holy Land*

Baron Ranulf will be back in two weeks time and Aelis will be with him. Her new husband is still in his mother's care. George is still in York. My guts still grumble. It is still cold.

28TH DAY OF JANUARY, *Feast of Saint John the Sage, an Irish philosopher who was stabbed to death by his students*

Last night we had sleeping in our hall two monks from the abbey on their way to Rome. God, it seems, told their abbot that He wants the remains of two Roman martyrs brought from Rome to a new home in the abbey church. Brother Norbert and Brother Behrtwald are going to Rome to find them. Rome is so far away that they will not return until harvest.

I thought to go with them but this morning when they left the snow was so deep and the wind so fierce and the dark so very dark that I snuggled down into my quilt and decided to wait for an adventure on some warmer day.

29TH DAY OF JANUARY, *Feast of Saint Julian the Hospitaler, who accidentally killed both his mother and father and in his grief and remorse built a hospital for the poor. Patron of innkeepers, boatmen, and travelers*

Peppercorn the dog is possessed of a demon. She howls and moans, digging at her head, running though the hall, rubbing her face on the straw. Morwenna has made a charm which I wet with spit and tied about her head (the dog's, not Morwenna's). I pray the demon leaves Peppercorn without entering anyone else.

31ST DAY OF JANUARY, *Feast of Saint Maedoc of Ferns, who lived seven years on barley bread and water*

We have taken all the Christmas greens down. The hall looks so gloomy and bare. It is still cold but thanks to God most of the lambs are still alive.

# FEBRUARY ✙

1ST DAY OF FEBRUARY, *Feast of Saint Brigid of Ireland, who turned her bathwater into beer for visiting monks*

Morwenna's charm did not help Peppercorn so we sent for Father Huw, but he refuses to work miracles on dogs. My father says he cannot stand the howling and running and digging, so he has sent Peppercorn to Rhys from the stables to be killed. I convinced Rhys to let Perkin take her. Dogs are much like goats—mayhap Perkin can help her.

3RD DAY OF FEBRUARY, *Feast of Saint Ia, who sailed across the Irish Sea on a leaf*

I am locked in my chamber this day for my rudeness to Fulk, the fat and flabby son of the baron Fulk from Normandy. It was like this: Yestermorn my father received a messenger from Baron Fulk, saying the baron would be here by noon to discuss further betrothal arrangements between the younger Fulk and myself. By cock and pie, I swore, I will not be given in marriage against my will! But I again hid in the privy to watch their arrival since I thought not to refuse right away if the young Fulk seemed clever or funny.

When you mix flour and salt and yeast and water to make the dough for bread and put it in a warm place, it swells, growing white and soft and spongy. That is what the young Fulk looked like. God's thumbs! No wonder the baron was willing to consider an alliance with a knight's daughter.

I stayed in that privy until Morwenna, seeking to rid herself of her breakfast ale before dinner, found me. Marched into the hall, I sulked through lamb cooked with raisins and two kinds of fruit tart. I frowned through the dancing. I scowled through the minstrel's songs.

After dinner, my father and the baron went to play chess, my mother to take a nap, Morwenna to the solar, the young Fulk to the stables, and myself back to the privy. Soon, though, I heard the rubbing and bouncing of too much flesh approaching and looked out. Young Fulk was coming. I sneaked out without being seen and he took my place on the privy seat. So I set fire to the privy.

By the bones of Saint Wigbert, I swear it was not intentional. Hoping to make flabby Fulk uncomfortable by filling the privy with foul-smelling smoke, I set afire a mound of wet hay nearby. Mayhap too nearby, for the privy soon was ablaze.

I did not intend the privy to burn. I did not intend the door to stick. I did not intend that the billowing smoke and Fulk's bellowing would bring most of the manor to help. I did not intend that when he finally did get out, it would be without his breeches. God's thumbs, his backside was the size of the millpond!

After the laughter and the joking and the dousing of the fire, I, of course, was caught and blamed. Morwenna and my father never even asked if I intended to do it. I was smacked and sent to my chamber. The two Fulks left without a betrothal. Rhys, John, and Wat must build a new privy.

4TH DAY OF FEBRUARY, *Feast of Saint Gilbert of Lincolnshire, furniture maker and founder of monasteries*

Peppercorn is back at home! Perkin found not a demon in her head but a candied fig in her ear. The fig is out and Peppercorn is herself again.

My mother took advantage of my merry spirits to speak of young Fulk and the privy fire. I knew it was coming. First was a lecture on courtesy to one's guests. Then obedience to one's father. Finally, the familiar talk about ladylike behavior—moderate in speech and laughter, discreet in word and deed. Corpus bones!

I said, "I am truly sorry, lady, that Rhys and John and Wat were put to the trouble of a new privy. I am sorry I disappointed you. But I would not wed the fat and flabby Fulk and would probably set him afire again."

"In truth," she said, "the baron Fulk left without a betrothal not because of your fire but because your father bested him at chess. I think your father would not humble himself before God Himself. Even to secure a baron's son for his daughter."

Then she sighed. I smiled. It is good to know that I have my father's pride as well as his beastliness to help me avoid this marriage business.

5TH DAY OF FEBRUARY, *Feast of Saint Agatha, who refused to wed the consul Quintinian and so was tortured by rods, rack, and fire and finally had her breasts cut off. I think I can understand a little her dilemma*

My mother is with child again. My father smirks and pats her swelling belly and already toasts to his son.

It does not seem to me that we need another babe. My mother said children are gifts from God, even though they sometimes seem like penance, and that as God's gifts we must welcome them.

"I also like the sweet, milky way they smell," she said. "And how they twine their arms about your neck and leave sticky kisses on your cheek."

I myself like dogs better.

What if this time God takes her as well as the babe? I am sore afraid.

6TH DAY OF FEBRUARY, *Feast of Saint Dorothy, a virgin martyr who sent back a basket of fruit from the Garden of Paradise, and celebration of the founding of our village church, Saint Dorothy's, one hundred seven years ago*

This might become my favorite feast day if we could celebrate it each year as we did today. First we heard a special Mass, which meant it was twice as long and my mind wandered twice as much and my knees got twice as tired.

After, we all gathered in the hall to eat, feasting on pig's stomach stuffed with nuts and apples, herring with parsnips, and a disgusting peacock, stuffed and roasted with his tail feathers stuck back on.

There was abundant wine as well as ale and cider and perry and we grew quite rowdy as we played Hoodman's Blind. The shallow-brained Lady Margaret, whenever it was her turn to be blindfolded, whiffled here and there around the hall and then wandered into the pantry, whereupon all the young men would follow her and none return to the game for minutes. Corpus bones! What an odd way to play!

Suddenly there was a commotion as two of my father's men pulled out their swords and started slashing at each other, each accusing the other of sneaking peeks over the blindfold. Everyone moved aside as Richard and Gilbert, cursing and grunting, swung their terrible heavy swords at each other. Up on the tables, where they overturned cups and goblets and stepped in and out of the plates of meat.

Onto the benches, which splintered as they swung and missed each other. Over to the walls, where their sharpened weapons cut new rends in the already tattered hangings.

All afternoon they swung until finally they were near too tired to lift their heavy weapons again. Gilbert heaved one last swipe at Richard, which knocked him off his feet. Bellowing about who did what unfairly to whom, their friends joined in, shouting and cursing and grunting along. Then we all joined in, even the cooks and servers swinging their ladles and pothooks. I with no weapon hurled food at whoever was near, pretending I was a crusader battling the heathens with leftover pig's stomach and almond cream.

One group of fighters stumbled into the fire, scattering the burning brands and smoldering ashes into the rushes, which burst into flame. Suddenly the hall floor was ablaze, as the dry rushes caught fire. Even William Steward's shoes were smoldering. William and Gilbert grabbed flagons of wine to pour over the blazing rushes while Richard stamped on the stray sparks and my father, the genius, pulled down his breeches and pissed most of the fire out. The hot fire seemed to cool our tempers, so everyone sat down to drink again amidst the ruins of the table and argue over which side got the better of the other. If I become a saint, I would like my day to be celebrated in just such fashion.

8TH DAY OF FEBRUARY, *Feast of Saint Cuthman, a hermit and beggar who took his crippled mother everywhere with him in a wheelbarrow*

I spent yesterday doctoring ale head, grumbling guts, and various cuts, gashes, scratches, and burns—including my own. Then just before dinner we found Roger Moreton lying unconscious in the black soggy rushes near the buttery. He sustained a grievous injury in the fight and lay untended all night while we slept. Now he lies in the solar in my parents' bed, still asleep, with cobwebs packed about his wound, his fever raging.

9TH DAY OF FEBRUARY, *Feast of Saint Apollonia, who relieves those suffering from toothache*

Roger's wound has grown black and smells bad. My mother and Morwenna and I do all we can, but his head is no better and his fever no less and his eyes still closed.

10TH DAY OF FEBRUARY, *Feast of Saint Scholastica, the first nun*

Roger died this morning. He never woke up. He was seventeen.

11TH DAY OF FEBRUARY, *Feast of Saint Gobnet, virgin and beekeeper*

Today is Roger's funeral ale, and our hall rings with noise and music and fighting and eating and drinking just as it did the day our brawling killed him. This will go on all night until the funeral Mass tomorrow after which there will be more feasting. I am in my chamber, for my head aches and my heart grieves, and I have no appetite for food, merriment, or company.

13TH DAY OF FEBRUARY, *Feast of Saint Modomnoc, who first brought bees to Ireland*

I told Morwenna that my hands were too cold for embroidery. She now watches me like a chicken hawk to make sure they are also too cold for writing. No more now.

14TH DAY OF FEBRUARY, *Feast of Saint Valentine, a Roman priest martyred on the Flaminian Way*

Today being the day birds choose their mates, I watched my birds all morning to see if I could spy them pairing off but they are acting just the same as always, so I must have missed it. Mating is definitely in season, however. Meg from the dairy giggles as she carries the milk pails and leaves a trail of spilled milk from here to there. The cook spent the forenoon teaching Wat's yellow-haired daughter to stir a porridge. Half the kitchen boys have disappeared with half the serving maids. And my father stopped blustering long enough to lay a kiss on my lady mother's head.

As we wove cloth this day, Morwenna and I talked of mating, love, and marriage. I told her I thought it all silly and a waste of time and if I were king I would outlaw it.

"Even the king would have trouble enforcing that law, Birdy," she said, "for one stick won't make fire, and God's creatures dearly love to warm their hands on a fire."

She laughed and snickered so to herself then that I could not get a word of sense out of her. God's thumbs. Mating season has soddened even Morwenna's wits.

16TH DAY OF FEBRUARY, *Feast of Saint Juliana, who argued with the Devil*

I am to go to Castle Finbury to visit the duchess of Warrington—the lady Aelis that was. She is there at home while she waits for her husband to grow up. I will be with her for fourteen days! My belly is quivering with excitement and a little still with remorse. I will take with me plenty of remedies.

18TH DAY OF FEBRUARY, *Feast of Saint Eudelme of Little Sodbury, about whom nothing is known except that she was a saint and I do not know how we even know that*

Just before dinner, Morwenna and I and our escorts arrived at Aelis's castle. Clattering over the moat bridge, we passed through the main gate into the castle yard. The castle seemed like a small stone city. Huddled against the great curtain wall with its stone towers were buildings of all sizes—a slope-roofed storage shed, a kitchen with a chimney like a church steeple, the great hall, a brewhouse, thatched barns and stables, a piggery, a smithy, and the chapel.

The yard teemed with sights and sounds. Great snorting horses coming or going or just milling around stirred the rain and snow and dirt into a great muddy slop. Peasants held wiggling, squawking ducks and chickens by their feet, shaking them in the face of anyone who might buy. Laundresses stirred great vats of dirty clothes in soapy water like cooks brewing up some gown-and-breeches stew. Bakers ran back and forth from the ovens at the side of the yard to the kitchen with great baskets of steamy fresh bread. Masons chipped stones and mixed mortar as they continued their everlasting repairs. Everywhere children tumbled over each other and everyone else, stealing bread, chasing dogs, splashing and slopping through the mud.

As we drew near to the great hall, the smells overpowered even the noise—the sour smell of the sick, the poor, and the old who crowded about the door, waiting for scraps of food or linen, the rotten sweet smell of the garbage and soiled rushes piled outside the kitchen door, and above all the smell of crisping fat and boiling meat and the hundreds of spices and herbs and honeys and wines that together make a castle dinner.

The great hall seemed larger than our whole manor at Stonebridge, and the tables were laid with enough golden plate to make my father die of greed were he but to see it. Dinner was festive, with wine and musicians and minstrels and much laughter. And food such as we see at home only for a feast, and never in winter—eels in quince jelly, hedgehog in raisins and cream, porpoise and peas, spun sugar castles, boats, and dragons—but I noticed that many of the dishes had snow on them, for the kitchens are outside in the yard and food must be carried through the snow to the hall.

After dinner Aelis and I walked about the castle yard for a few minutes, but it was too cold, so we ducked into the kennels to see her new hounds. A stable boy not more than ten years old sleeps there to see to their needs—how thin and cold he looked. The dogs were cleaner and better fed. I gave him some cheese and bread I had concealed in my sleeve for later, for I did not relish crossing the yard in the middle of the night to steal food from the kitchens the way I do at home.

Aelis, now that she is married, wears her hair tied up in bunches over each ear but she still gossips like the old unmarried Aelis. She wanted to talk about George but I was pricked with guilt and tried to talk about anything else. She said she sent him a message and although he never responded, she will love him until she dies. Prick. Prick.

19TH DAY OF FEBRUARY, *Feast of Saint Olran, who was Saint Patrick's chariot driver*

The night sounds in a castle are so different from home. I could barely sleep for the clanking and calling of the guards as they passed one another in the night, the laughter and shouting of the guests still drinking in the hall, and the loud, sharp sound of footsteps on stone, unmuffled by dirt and rushes.

The castle was abustle early this day with cooking and sweeping and the mucking out of privies. A messenger had arrived to say that the king's cousin, Madame Joanna, will stop here to rest on her way from York to London. She is but two or three days away!

Aelis and I have been hiding from all the activity so that no one will think of something for us to do. We are guessing what the great lady is like. Aelis imagines she is tall like the king, slender as a weasel, and white as whale's bone, dressed in cloth of gold and sea-green velvet, with jewels instead of keys hanging from the belt at her waist. So says Aelis.

I think she is clever and funny and writes songs. And that she will grow to love me and not wish to be without me and will take me with her to London to the king's palace where we will dance every night until morning and have adventures and many knights will love us and even wish to die for us, but we will have none! If we wish to be puppeteers at a fair or skate on the ice or be strolling players, we will, for who could refuse the cousin of the king and her beloved friend? And I will never again have to spin or weave or comb wool or stir boiling vats of anything! And no one will be able to marry me off for silver or land. I cannot wait until she arrives, friendly and kind and beautiful as summer.

I have brushed and smoothed my best green gown and Aelis will let me wear her lavender surcoat over it to hide the worst stains. I washed my hair and near roasted my backside at the fire trying to get it dry. My shoes are cleaned and my fingernails also. I must be at my best for this opportunity.

20TH DAY OF FEBRUARY, *Feast of Saint Wulfric of Haselbury, a hermit who doused himself frequently with cold water for penance*

All is ready but Madame Joanna has not yet arrived. Aelis and I are huddled beneath the bed covers trying to keep warm while I write. There are icicles on the walls of her chamber, on the side away from the fire. I thought great barons and their families lived in luxury, but this castle is much wetter and colder than Stonebridge Manor. The fleas are the same as at home, although the wine is better.

Two villagers and a goat froze to death last night. Where is my dear Madame?

21ST DAY OF FEBRUARY, *Feast of Saint Peter Damian, monk, cardinal, poet, and maker of wooden spoons*

Madame Joanna arrived this day while we were at dinner. The baron hurried out of the hall to greet her and bring her in. I was taken greatly by surprise. She is a hundred years old, gray and puny, smaller even than Robin Smallbone's sister, who is not yet eight. Her face is all wrinkled and brown and covered with gray hairs, her eyes are round and red, and she is missing all her teeth but the front two on top. God's thumbs, I thought, Madame Mouse.

I watched her closely during dinner. Her veil and wimple were crooked and stained with crumbs and gravy from her attempts to straighten them. When she talked or ate, which she mostly did at the same time, she lisped and whistled so no one could understand her at all. A tiny dog who looked like a hairy beetle sat on her lap all through dinner. She fed him the best pieces of meat picked from the serving bowls. Sometimes the dog sniffed or licked a piece of meat and then would not eat it, so she'd put it back in the bowl. No one dared chide her, her being the cousin of the king!

Was this the beloved friend, beautiful as summer, who would rescue me and take me to court where we would dance and frolic? Disappointment grumbled my guts and made my breath sour.

After dinner Madame Joanna told fortunes. It was hard to know what she said, for she talked in riddles and proverbs while lisping and whistling, but those who thought they heard of love left blushing and giggling and those who thought they heard of riches grinned, so most seemed pleased.

My turn came and I near fainted when she said, "Come closer, Little Bird." How could she know that name? She peered intently into my face, her mouth so close her whistling tickled my chin.

Finally she said, "You are lucky, Little Bird, for you

have wings. But you must learn to master them. Look at the baron's hawk there on her perch. Just because she doesn't flap her wings all the time doesn't mean she can't fly."

I was impressed with her knowing Little Bird but could make little sense of the soothsaying. I went to bed.

22ND DAY OF FEBRUARY, *Feast of Saint Baradates, called The Admirable, it does not say why*

The sun came out fiercely this day and warms the world. After dinner the baron took a party out hawking although it is early in the year, for they said they could not waste this glorious day. They will spend the afternoon setting birds to hunt and kill other birds. You can imagine what I think about that. Aelis has gone with them.

After dreaming in the sun a while, I wandered into the hall and found Madame Joanna there, eating boiled cabbage and bacon at the great table, all alone except for her dog. She called me over, bade me sit, and fed me bits of bacon just as she did the dog. She said I reminded her of her youngest daughter, who is now a queen in some German country, so we talked about her children. She tries to be kind to them, she said, but on the whole prefers her dog.

And we talked about me. I told her about Stonebridge and Perkin—she agreed he sounds quite superior for a goat boy—and Morwenna and my father and the endless business of learning to be the lady of the manor, the spinning, embroidering, hemming, brewing, doctoring, combing, marrying, and on and on. I told her of my dreamings about her and going back to court with her where we would have adventures and do exactly as we pleased.

"Adventures!" she squeaked. "I am a woman and cousin to the king. Do you truly think I could be a horse trainer or a puppeteer or even be friends with a goat boy? Do you think I have adventures instead of duties? There are many worse chores than spinning, Little Bird.

"But, my dear," she went on, "I flap my wings at times, choose my fights carefully, get things done, understand my limitations, trust in God and a few people, and here I am. I survive, and sometimes even enjoy."

She smiled then, a lovely smile except for the cabbage stuck between her only two teeth. "You," she added, "must learn about wings, my dear."

And then, before I could ask what she meant, the bird killers returned, tables were laid for supper, and my time to charm the king's cousin was over.

24TH DAY OF FEBRUARY, *Feast of Saint Matthias, who preached to cannibals*

I did not see Madame Joanna again, for I was called home all unwilling to celebrate the marriage of the abominable Robert to the little heiress of Foxbridge. They have been handfast for two years and were to have been married in two more when she reached fourteen. Robert promised not to bed with her while she was of such a tender age, but from the looks of her, he paid no more attention to his promise than a cow at Mass. Either the girl has overfed herself on honey cakes or the child is with child.

Her father is too angry with them to risk letting them go to Foxbridge, so we will have the wedding here. My father, Sir Nip-Cheese, objects to the cost, saying it is obvious they are already husband and wife. My mother in her quiet way does as she wishes. Robert and his bride will have a hasty but real wedding and we will get all the meat eaten before Lent begins.

26TH DAY OF FEBRUARY, *Feast of Saint Ethelbert of Kent, first English king to become a Christian*

The wedding feast still rollicks below, but I have had my fill of merriment and have escaped to my chamber to write this account of the day's events.

The morning started out gray and drizzly, with a mist that wet our faces and our clothes and made the rushlights hard to fire, a poor omen for a wedding. We dressed the bride in her second-best gown (Morwenna let the seams out) and on her hair put a small veil held with a golden band.

The musicians came at dawn, yawning and scratching, smelling of the sour wine they had drunk half the night. On bagpipe and crumhorn they played us to the church.

Robert and his bride exchanged vows at the

church door and we all went inside for Mass, a lengthy affair with priest droning and candles hissing and flickering. The loudest sound was the musicians snoring. I think Robert fell asleep himself but was jostled awake by my father's sharp elbow.

I watched the early morning light pass over and through the windows of colored glass, leaving streaks of red and green and yellow on the stone floor. When I was little, I used to try to capture the colored light. I thought I could hold it in my hand and carry it home. Now I know it is like happiness—it is there or it is not, you cannot hold it or keep it.

We walked back to the manor for the ale feast, showering the bride with rose petals, the musicians playing and tomfooling. Gerd the miller's son fell into the river as we crossed, but Robert waded in and pulled him out so his wedding day would not be ruined.

The dark and smoky hall looked festive for the feast. The rushes on the floor were last year's but were new strewn with mint and heather. Tables were laid with our best linen cloths. Torches blazed in iron brackets on the wall and their light gleamed off the gilt and silver goblets, candlesticks, and spoons. I have seldom seen these—what has not been sold is usually locked up.

After dinner, the men all danced with the bride. She looked smaller and paler as the day wore on but bravely let every man there step on her feet and call it dancing.

I was partnered for the feast with an ugly shaggy-bearded hulk from the north. My father sought to honor him because his manor lies next to my mother's, and my father lusts after it. I fail to see how sitting next to me and sharing my bowl and goblet honored him—and it certainly did me no good. The man was a pig, which dishonors pigs. He blew his red and shiny nose on the table linen, sneezed on the meat, picked his teeth with his knife, and left wet greasy marks where he drank from the cup we shared. I could not bring myself to put my lips to the slimy rim, so endured a dinner without wine.

Worse than this, he proved himself near a murderer. As the dogs burrowed under the rushes for bones and bits of the wedding meat, Rosemary (the smallest and my favorite but for Brutus) mistook his skinny foot for a bone and nipped it. The shaggy-bearded pig howled and kicked the dog, who, of course, defended herself by biting. Then Shaggy Beard, pulling his knife from the table, tried to skewer the dog as if she were a joint of meat.

Robert left his wine cup long enough to knock the knife away with his. "The dog belongs to Lord Rollo," he growled, "and is not yours to kill."

The bearded pig sat down, shamed before our guests, and began to eat and drink again, smiling at me with meat stuck between his horrible brown broken teeth. I think he ate too much, for he made wind like a storm and sounded like a bladderpipe left out in the rain played by a goat.

The worst part is that now I must be beholden to the abominable Robert. As we passed later, I thanked him—prettily, I thought. He pinched my rump and grinned. "So I am none so bad as you thought me, little sister?"

I said, "Even the lowest of beasts is not vile all of the time."

I felt better. We are now back on the old footing — hate.

27TH DAY OF FEBRUARY, *Shrove Tuesday and the Feast of Saint Alnoth, serf and cowherd*

Today my father questioned me about the bearded pig. I said he affected my stomach like maggoty meat and my father laughed and said, "Learn to like it."

It bodes not well. Shaggy Beard has a son, Stephen, whom he spoke of with loathing, calling him "Sir Priest," "the clerk," and "the girl," because the boy thinks and bathes and does not fart at Mass. I fear they are planning a match between me and Stephen. I will not. To be part of Shaggy Beard's family and have to eat with him every day! If my father does not drive him away, I will, as I have done the others.

28TH DAY OF FEBRUARY, *Ash Wednesday*

First day of Lent. We are but dust and to dust shall return. I tried to be thoughtful and morbid on this day but spoiled it by skipping in the yard after dinner from pure joy. I am not dust yet!

Shaggy Beard is with us still. When I see him, I call "Hoy!" as if I were calling a pig. His face gets even redder. I am hoping he will burst and we can sweep him out with the soiled rushes.

# March ✠

Robert is wedded and bedded—again—and he and his bride have left for her own manor at Ashton, not long ahead of her father, Robert fears. My mother and her women like it not that Robert's pale puny bride, so far gone with child, is jouncing and bouncing over the fens, but Robert thinks her father in his anger will try to keep the new-wed couple from the manor promised to the girl. So they race across Britain in the rain.

When I marry it will be no cheap rag-tag hurry-up affair as Robert's was. I will have silks and music and lights and important guests from foreign lands with musical names. I will braid my hair with silken threads and wear a gown of saffron silk with a red cloak and purple leather shoes embroidered with gold and silver threads. My belt will have bells on it and thin pieces of gold beaten into the shape of leaves and flowers. My betrothed, in a cloak of scarlet silk, will meet me at my father's house. His horses will have flowers and ribbons woven into their manes and their saddles draped with silk. Musicians, sober and well shod, will lead us to the church playing on silver flutes and gitterns, on timbrels and cymbals and lyres. It will sound like angels laughing and spring rain.

2ND DAY OF MARCH, *Feast of Saint Chad, whose dust taken in water cures men and cows of their infirmities and restores them to health*

The weather has warmed and the fleas have come to visit. This morning I gathered alder leaves with dew on them and strewed them about my chamber to discourage the black soldiers. I have forty-three bites, only twenty-seven of them in places I can easily scratch.

3RD DAY OF MARCH, *Feast of Saint Cunegund, wife to the emperor Henry. The little book of saints says that Cunegund once slapped her niece for frivolity and the finger-marks remained on her face until death. I am fortunate that no one in this household is a saint or I would be marked like a spotted horse, especially my cheeks and my rump*

No further words from my father about Shaggy Beard, so mayhap the trouble has passed and these plans, too, come to nothing.

4TH DAY OF MARCH, *Feast of Saint Adrian (the Irish one, not the African)*

We heard Mass this morning, or rather did not hear it, for the raindrops pounding on the church roof made a noise like drummers in a funeral procession and I heard nothing else. The church seems strange, undressed as it is for Lent. Father Huw wears plain robes with no silver gilt threads. The cross and statues are covered with veils. There are no flowers and no music. It is meant to make us feel sad, but mostly just makes me bored.

Edward has sent to us three holy books from which he says we must read each night during Lent to put us in the proper morose and holy mood. I was excited to have them, thinking they must be like the lively colorful little book of saints from the abbot. But then William Steward began to read, droning and stumbling over the Latin. Tonight's book is Saint Jerome. It is not lively or colorful. I hope it is short.

6TH DAY OF MARCH, *Feast of Saint Conon, martyr and maintainer of irrigation canals*

I have been gathering violets to make oil of violets against attacks of melancholy. Since I turned thirteen last year I have used a great amount of oil of violets.

7TH DAY OF MARCH, *Feast of Saint Perpetua, who turned into a man and trod on the Devil's head*

I hate Lent already and it has only been a seven-night.

8TH DAY OF MARCH, *Feast of Saint Duthac, who had miraculous powers to cure ale head*

Thomas of Wallingham and his family are stopping here on their way to London for Easter. His daughter is dull and proper and I would ordinarily shun her, but Lent is so dreary, I welcome even Agnes as an amusement.

Perched on the edge of my bed, Agnes, with her little black eyes and pointed nose, looked like a weasel in blue silk. But remembering the boredom that is Lent, I tried nicely to engage her.

Gossip she would not. Too hurtful.

Tell stories she would not. Too fanciful.

Dance she would not. Too frivolous.

"Let us then," I said, "go watch John Swann unload kegs at the alehouse."

"Why?" she asked.

"Because he is beautiful as summer and his arms ripple like the muscles on a horse's back and the rain plasters his shirt against his chest."

"The beauty of men and women is but the devil's work," she said, pinching her mouth like a fish. "A snare and a delusion. A trap for the innocent."

Innocent? Me? I was insulted by the thought. I who have seen a hanging, chased young Fulk from the privy, seen my birds in mating season and Perkin's goats!

When I got to the goats, Agnes covered her ears and ran squealing from my chamber. I miss Aelis.

9TH DAY OF MARCH, *Feast of Saint Bosa, monk of Whitby, bishop of York, and great-great-great-grand-father of Elfa the laundress*

Like a weasel, Agnes of Wallingham snorts in her sleep. She took all the covers and her feet are cold, her knees and ankles sharp as stones. And she does not leave until tomorrow.

It rained this day, so I could not escape outside. I spent the afternoon in the kitchen with Cuthman Cook, who was chopping eel for pies. He was telling me of the time he seduced the miller's daughter and had to hide in a barrel of flour and how the angry miller followed him home by following his floury footprints and I was laughing loudly when the heavy curtain was pushed aside and there was The Weasel, having sniffed me out.

"Your noise is offensive to well-mannered ears," she said. "It is said, 'A silent woman is always more admired than a noisy one.'"

"It is also said, 'A woman's tongue is her sword,'" I countered, "'and she does not let it rust.'"

"'Maids should be mild and meek, swift to hear and slow to speak,'" said Agnes.

"'Be she old or be she young, a woman's strength is in her tongue,'" said I.

Agnes pointed her nose at me. "'One tongue is enough for two women.'"

Having run out of sayings to argue with, I pushed her and she sat hard in the eel pie. Am I at fault because she has no balance? Being sent to my chamber at least meant I did not have to see her at supper.

As Morwenna led me out by my ear, The Weasel snuffled and said, "Violence, Catherine, becomes you as ill as that dress you are wearing," and then began to argue with the cook about the pie crust. God's thumbs, the girl would quarrel even with the breeze.

10TH DAY OF MARCH, *Feast of the Forty Martyrs of Sebaste, soldiers of the Thundering Legion, who were killed by being stranded on a frozen lake*

Thomas of Wallingham and his family continued on their way to London today. I think on the whole Agnes is more dreary even than Lent.

11TH DAY OF MARCH, *Feast of Saint Oengus the Culdee, an Irish bishop who genuflected frequently and recited the psalms while standing in cold water*

At Mass today I wondered instead of listening to the sermon, but they were wonderings about holy things, so I trust God was not offended. First I wondered why, after Lazarus was raised from the dead, people did not ask him about heaven and hell and being dead. Were they not curious? Indeed, this may have been our only chance to find out without dying.

Then I wondered why Jesus used his miraculous powers to cure lepers instead of creating an herb or flower that would cure them so we could continue to use it even now when Jesus is in Heaven. When we are on the road, I hate to hear the bell of a leper hiding in the trees until we pass. I know priests say lepers are paying for their great sins, but I know plenty of great sinners who still have their fingers and noses.

And I wondered about how long it took Noah to gather up two of everything for the Ark. The rain was pouring down and his family were driving bears and dogs and horses aboard and old Noah was in the garden catching flies and gnats, digging for worms and dung beetles and maggots. Why did he bother? Did he worry that he got all of them? Were there some disgusting slimy creeping things that Noah never found and so we do not have anymore?

13TH DAY OF MARCH, *Feast of Saint Mochoemoc, called also MoChamhog, Kennoch, Kevoca, Pulcherius, and Vulcanius, an abbot who could raise the dead to life*

I have been two days locked in my chamber. How it happened was this: In these dreary, deadly dull days of Lent, are we not told to make our own humble amusements? I therefore declared a contest to see who could spit the farthest: Rhys from the stables, Gerd the miller's son, William Steward's youngest son William, or me. I did not think to be left out just because I am a girl.

I did not win, Rhys did. His front teeth being loose since a fight with John Swann at the alehouse, he can spit between them at great distance and with deadly accuracy. We did not intend that my mother's ladies should be passing at that very moment or that they should mind spit so very much.

I was sent to my chamber without supper. Before I left, I declared, "I do not remember Our Blessed Lord ever condemning spitting. He did not make it a deadly sin like pride or gluttony or greed." Here I looked meaningfully at my father. "In fact," I continued, "did not Our Lord Himself once mix spittle with clay to heal a man of blindness?"

I thought it quite an eloquent argument. What it won me was another day in my chamber, *without* my inks.

14TH DAY OF MARCH, *Feast of Saint Matilda, persecuted by her children for generosity*

There is a new boy here for fostering, although who would trust their son to my father's care I cannot imagine. He looks to be about my age and is comely enough from afar. I will ask his name.

15TH DAY OF MARCH, *Feast of Saint Longinus, the soldier who pierced the side of the crucified Christ with his lance. Christ's blood cured his blindness, so he became a Christian and a monk, had his teeth knocked out and his tongue cut out, and died. My uncle George once saw his lance in a church in Antioch*

Geoffrey! Geoffrey! Geoffrey!

16TH DAY OF MARCH, *Feast of Saint Finnian the Leper,* *abbot of the Monastery of Swords*

Each time I tried to write of Geoffrey yestereve, I swooned and could not control my hands. He is not just comely but as beautiful as an angel, with golden hair and blue eyes and the habit of catching his lower lip between his teeth that makes me want to lie on the rushes and sigh. I stared boldly at him as he served my father at dinner yesternoon, but he looked only at the floor. I must take care always to wear my best shoes.

17TH DAY OF MARCH, *Feasts of Saint Patrick, apostle* *to Ireland, and Saint Gertrude, who protects us from rats*

A kinsman of my mother arrived today to celebrate Easter week. He is called Odd William to distinguish him from William Steward and Brother William at the abbey. He is writing a history of the world in Welsh and has been for all the fourteen years I have known him, living first with one cousin and then another, all across England. He is gray. His hair is gray, his eyes gray, and the rest of him stringy and gray. We housed him all last summer and he looks to stay this time until Christmas.

At least he does not sleep in my chamber but in the hall for the warmth, and it is his habit to write there, too, back to the fire, day after day, so that the back of his gown is all pocked with burn holes, like Sym's face after the spotted fever. My mother kindly pretends that he is a great man. The rest of us usually overlook him, ofttimes stumbling into and over him as if he were some invisible obstacle.

18TH DAY OF MARCH, *Feast of Saint Edward, king of England, killed by his wicked stepmother, who was very beautiful and became a nun*

Still Lent. No feasts, fairs, or visiting minstrels. No almond custard or roasts of beef. No singing, no dancing, just eating fish, listening to Jerome, and feeling sad until Easter. I have made a Lenten song:

> *Gray Lent comes bringing Jesus' doom.*
> *Church and hall are filled with gloom.*
> *Chant silently of sorrow.*

> *Forty days of feeling sad*
> *About the pain that Jesus had.*
> *Hum quietly till morrow.*

> *On the Cross the Christ hangs slain*
> *But promises to come again.*
> *Sing bright like a boy.*

> *Lenten ends with Easter Day.*
> *Off with black, put on the gay.*
> *Shout loudly of joy!*

I wanted to end with lines about hope but can think of no rhymes but rope, soap, pope, and mope, and none of these seem to fit the song. I think Lent is all about hope. No matter how bad we feel about Jesus dying or how sick we get of fish, Easter Day always comes. We just need to hope and believe.

There are new kittens in the barn.

19TH DAY OF MARCH *Feast of Saint Joseph, foster father of Jesus, husband of Mary, patron of carpenters and fathers*

A messenger arrived this night for the beast my father. From Murgaw, lord of Lithgow, the shaggy-bearded pig of the wedding feast. My father has said nothing to me yet, but I fear it is a request for me to wed and bed with Shaggy Beard's son. I will not. God's thumbs! Is there no end to this procession of unsuitable suitors? Perhaps I should ask Thomas Carpenter to help me construct a trap door in the hall and just drop them into the river as they arrive.

20TH DAY OF MARCH, *Feast of Saint Cuthbert, whose body remains undecayed five hundred years after his death*

Shaggy Beard has not asked for me to marry his son. It is Shaggy Beard himself who wishes to take me for wife! What a monstrous joke. That dog assassin whose breath smells like the mouth of Hell, who makes wind like others make music, who attacks helpless animals with knives, who is ugly and old!

My father called me into the solar this morning. He was smiling. I knew it meant no good for me.

"My beloved daughter," he said.

Trouble, I knew. "Who?" I said. "I am your daughter, God help me, but hardly beloved. So who is it you address?"

He still smiled, so I knew the matter was serious. "My lady of Lithgow," he said. "Your bridegroom awaits you and none of your tricks will profit you this time."

Twenty words and a crack on the rump and I was out in the hall again, betrayed and betrothed. Lady Shaggy Beard. Good fortune and goodbye.

I must make a plan, for I will not, of course, wed the pig. Deus! I cannot even conceive of such a fate. Could it be? Would they really sell me to that odious old man? I cannot think so. I will contrive something. Luckily I am experienced at outwitting suitors.

21ST DAY OF MARCH, *Feast of the Martyrs of Alexandria, killed by a mob of angry heretics*

My mother lectured to me today on a daughter's duty, and she sees mine as marriage where my father wills. She has no great love for Murgaw the Shaggy Beard, but seems overcome by his title and his wealth and his land, so is no ally to me against my father. Leastwise she insists we make no further plans until Lent be over.

It seems so long ago that I wrote a Lenten song and spoke of hope and the promise of Easter Day. Now I would that Lent would last forever.

This morning, feeling trapped, I got it into my head to run away. I accept that I cannot be a monk—my chest is too big—or a crusader—my stomach is too weak—but there must be something I can do.

I ran to Perkin on the meadow to help me unriddle this. I said, "Perkin, I must escape or be Lady Shaggy Beard until I die. I am thinking to run away and be a puppeteer at a fair."

Perkin said, "You tangle your spinning. You tangle your weaving. You would tangle the puppet strings. You cannot be a puppeteer."

"A wandering singer," I said.

Perkin said, "Remember the monk who tried to escape from the terrible King John by disguising himself as a minstrel although he couldn't sing, and how he was found out and hanged by his thumbs until they grew as long as a mule's ears? When you sing, it sounds like someone slammed a door on a goat's tail. You cannot be a wandering singer."

"A wart charmer," I said.

Perkin said, "You must first have the talent to make warts fall off."

We tried it on the wart on his elbow. I do not have the talent.

"I could teach birds to talk," I said.

"Most people," he replied, "think there is already

more than enough talking in this world. You cannot teach birds to talk."

"I could have a booth at a fair and sell things," I said.

"What?" he said.

"Ribbons."

"Where would you get them?"

"Sausages."

"Who would make them?"

"My old clothes."

"Who would want them?"

I pinched him and went home. God's thumbs! Sometimes Perkin is so sensible it makes my gut wamble.

23RD DAY OF MARCH, *Feast of Saint Gwinear, who grew thirsty while hunting so struck the ground with his staff and three fountains sprang up, one for himself, one for his horse, and one for his dog. The Irish have always taken good care of their animals*

In the solar with my father this morning: "Daughters and fish spoil easily and are better not kept. You will, Lady Birdy, be wed. If this new suitor is stubborn enough to outlast your willfulness, he will be your husband. If not, I will find another, mayhap even less to your liking. Accept it."

Will I then be caught in this marriage trap? If I must be wed, I'd rather it be to someone young and comely like Geoffrey.

24TH DAY OF MARCH, *Feast of Saint Hildelith, Saxon princess and abbess of Barking*

Although it is Lent, I contrived a game of Squeak, Piggy, Squeak after dinner. I thought to find Geoffrey alone but instead was caught by Walter Rufus, grinning and making kissing noises. God's thumbs, this marriage business is very complicated.

25TH DAY OF MARCH, *Feast of Our Lady in Lent. First day of the new year*

It is 1291. I pray the new year brings us joy and wealth, that George comes back for Easter and that Robert does not, and that God assist me in this marriage matter.

26TH DAY OF MARCH, *Feast of Saint Liudger, bishop, denounced for excessive almsgiving*

Tonight I stayed awake for the holy book, for we read of all the ways martyrs have died for the glory of God: being disemboweled or boiled alive or skinned or eaten by lions or torn apart by the torture hook. Until the day of the Last Judgment, when all the dead shall be made whole again, Heaven must look like the abbey gate where the maimed and injured and crippled gather for bits of bread from the almoner. Morwenna says unless my behavior improves, I will never know.

27TH DAY OF MARCH, *Feast of Saint Rupert, bishop of*

Worms. I do not know why worms have their own bishop and other creatures do not

As it rained so hard this day, we sat by the fire and told stories. William Steward told of the nut-brown maid who fell in love with an outlaw and followed him to the woods to share even outlawry with him. I cried so hard I had to wipe my tears on the table linen, for my sleeves were drenched. I knew those feelings of devoted love and the desperate need to be free.

I saw Geoffrey near the door to the buttery, tears on his face, and knew he felt as I did. Mayhap we could be like the nut-brown maid and the outlaw, living in the forest beneath the sheltering trees, sleeping in each other's arms under the stars. Would Geoffrey follow me into the forest? If only he would look at me, I might read the answer in his eyes. Since he will not, I suppose I must ask him.

28TH DAY OF MARCH, *Feast of Saint Alkelda of Giggleswick, Saxon princess, strangled to death by Viking women*

Odd William says Worms is a place.

29TH DAY OF MARCH, *Feast of Saints Gwynllyw and Gwladys, who bathed in the river Usk summer and winter and went for long walks completely naked until their son, the holy Cadoc, made them stop*

It rains again. I have spent the morning in my

chamber making a new song:

> *Every face has eyes, I mark,*
> *Large or small, light or dark,*
> *Brown or green or in between,*
> *Black or gray or light as day,*
> *Or blue as the wing feathers of a lark.*

> *Why then do some eyes flash a light*
> *Turning darkness into bright,*
> *Saying words too proud to speak aloud,*
> *Haunting my dreams, or so it seems,*
> *Whether it be day or night?*

> *Why do some eyes make me want to shine,*
> *Become more gentle, true, and fine,*
> *Make of me what I best could be,*
> *Even when those eyes I so highly prize*
> *Have never once looked into mine?*

30TH DAY OF MARCH, *Feast of Saint Zosimus of Syracuse, renowned for being the last saint in my little book of saints*

As soon as he has wood and thatch for a cottage and her father has three pigs for her dowry, the oldest son of Thomas Baker will wed Meg from the dairy. He has been looking lustily after her for three years, since they were twelve and chased birds from the field together, and she finally looked back. Their fathers bickered, bargained, and agreed, so it is settled. They are very happy and giggle at each other when they pass on the road. Why can villagers have a say in whom they marry and I cannot? I wish I were a villager.

31ST DAY OF MARCH, *Feast of Saint Balbina the Virgin, maiden of Rome, buried on the Appian Way*

I am confounded. What should I be doing these days? Packing up what I will need living in the forest with Geoffrey? Refusing to eat until Shaggy Beard gives me up? Making another plan? Only two more weeks of Lent.

April ✠

1ST DAY OF APRIL, *All Fools Day and Feasts of Saints Walaric, Agilbert, and Tewdric*

After Mass, I sent Tom the kitchen boy for pigeon's milk and asked William Steward to order me striped paint. They just grunted. I asked Morwenna to help me gather hen's teeth but she says I ask her that every Fools Day and it has never yet fooled her. I spent the rest of the day sulking in the barn. The kittens have grown.

2ND DAY OF APRIL, *Feast of Saint Mary of Egypt, a female hermit who lived on berries and dates and was buried by a lion*

Mayhap I could be a hermit. I wonder what they do.

3RD DAY OF APRIL, *Feast of Saint Pancras of Taormina, stoned to death by brigands*

Morwenna is on a crusade to tidy me. I could not go out this day until I had brushed my hair eighty times. When I finished I pretended I was going to join my mother in the solar but instead took up a position in the hall from which I could see Geoffrey as he set up the table and benches for dinner. I plan to follow him every day until I know his heart, or at least can guess well enough, in this matter of following me into the forest.

4TH DAY OF APRIL, *Feast of Saint Isidore of Seville, archbishop and writer of books*

An unlucky discovery. Geoffrey looks like a hedgehog when he frowns. Mayhap he will grow out of it.

5TH DAY OF APRIL, *Feast of Saint Derfel, soldier and monk*

I am full weary tonight from following Geoffrey from hall to yard to village to stables to hall. It is more tiring to get from here to the stables by going behind the pig yard, around the dovecote, through the muck heap, and over the privy so that you cannot be seen than by just walking in a straight line from here to there.

Geoffrey, I have learned, is good at games and swordplay, meek and quiet when serving my father, better on a horse than the other boys. He is vain about his clothes, taking care to keep them clean and free of wrinkles, but he cannot read and does not wish to learn. He is polite to the bigger boys but not so kind to the little ones. He is not exactly like the Geoffrey of my dreaming.

6TH DAY OF APRIL, *Feast of Saint Brychan, who had sixty-three children*

I could not follow Geoffrey today until near supper, for I was caught by Morwenna this morning and made to do all the sheet-hemming I had not done these many days. Bones! I near wore out my fingers. But finally I finished and escaped to the yard where Geoffrey and the other boys were wrestling. Geoffrey had taken off his tunic and his shirt to keep them clean, and his body looked very beautiful in the sunshine. After, they all walked to the millpond to wash. I saw Geoffrey, with whom I was willing to share my life and my love and my freedom, hobbling about pretending to be Perkin while the other boys laughed.

In my fury I marched right up to him and for the first time looked into his eyes. God's thumbs, he looked like my brother Robert! One good shove sent Geoffrey and his beautiful body and his precious fine clothes into the millpond. I hope tonight when he takes off his breeches a dead fish falls out.

7TH DAY OF APRIL, *Feast of Saint Goran, a hermit who lived in a cave in Cornwall, which must have been so cold and damp that only a saint could do it, or a fairy, or perhaps a giant*

I am badly out of humor. I have lost the possibility of Geoffrey, I am no nut-brown maid who can live in the forest, and Shaggy Beard awaits me. Mayhap after all this time he has forgotten me and has moved on to torture some other girl with his unwanted affection. If not, I vow I will find a way to be rid of him. I will be no Lady Shaggy Beard.

I can think no more on this now, busy as we will be with Holy Week praying and fasting and chanting and weeping and holy books.

Corpus bones. I utterly loathe my life.

8TH DAY OF APRIL, *Palm Sunday, the entry of Jesus into Jerusalem*

The young people of the village went palming before dawn today to gather willow branches for the church. Most had more greenery stuck in their hair and clothes than in their baskets. I foresee a large crop of babies come next Christmas.

9TH DAY OF APRIL, *Feast of Saint Madrun, daughter of Vortimer, High King of the Britons*

This being the start of Holy Week, we now hear Mass every day and have two readings from a holy book. In between, I stole bread and cheese from the kitchen and ran outside. I could not let this first warm day of spring pass without my dancing in the meadow.

10TH DAY OF APRIL, *Tuesday of Holy Week and the Feast of Hedda of Peterborough, killed by the same savage Danes who killed King Edmund*

I noted as I climbed into my bed last night that Wat was trimming the rushlights. This morning, although I woke before dawn, the worst of the soot was cleaned from the fireplace, the cold ashes were gone, and a new fire was brightly crackling. It occurred to me that Wat had worked through much of the night and it also occurred to me that it had never before occurred to me. When does Wat enjoy the warmth of his bed?

11TH DAY OF APRIL, *Wednesday of Holy Week and the Feast of Saint Guthlac, hermit of Crowland, tempted by devils*

We have received a message from my uncle George. He is coming for a visit after Easter. Now I have two worries: this joke of a betrothal to Shaggy Beard, and my uncle George. Is he still drunk? Does he still mope? Has my curse really blighted his life? Will I need to make myself more remedies against guilt?

12TH DAY OF APRIL, *Maundy Thursday and the Feast of Saint Zeno of Verona, who liked to fish*

Today we began to read of the Passion and death of Our Lord. It is a sad and tragic story and I do not sleep through it but watch it in my mind like a play unfolding. I picture Jesus like my uncle George, and my mother as His blessed mother. The evil Judas in my mind looks like the miller, scrawny and scowling and mean. Herod is my father, and Pontius Pilate that Sir Lack-Wit who was once my suitor. The apostles look like our villagers except for Saint Peter, who is Morwenna in leggings and a tunic. Saint Peter seems so human and unlike a saint. I think he may be my favorite, although Saint John is as beautiful as summer—or Geoffrey.

13TH DAY OF APRIL, *Good Friday and the Feast of Saints Carpus, Papylus, and Agathonice, scraped with claws and burned to death*

This sad holy day we spent in church, marking the death of Our Lord. I wore my second-best kirtle so I would not ruin my best as we crept on the floor toward the altar. I don't know if that is fair to God but I do not believe He wants me to ruin the only good kirtle I own. I believe He likes me to look my best when I hear Mass.

14TH DAY OF APRIL, *Holy Saturday and the Feast of Saint Caradoc, a Welsh harper who lost his prince's grey-hounds and so became a monk*

My mother was not with us for the procession of Our Lord's coffin around the church. Being tortured with headaches and the bulk of the growing babe, she stayed abed with a tonic I made her of chamomile and honey. Her discomfort discomforts me.

15TH DAY OF APRIL, *Easter Day and the Feast of Saint Ruadhan, an Irish abbot who engaged in a cursing match with the pagan rulers of Tara and won*

Christ has risen! I got out of bed at dawn today so I could see the sun dance for joy as it is said to do each Easter. It rained, as it does each Easter.

The manor is full of guests celebrating the season, most of whom are sleeping in my chamber and my bed. I dream sometimes that I lie in bed and reach out my arms and fingers as wide as I can, and stretch my toes to the bottom of the bed, and do not touch anybody! And that I can get up and spin around my chamber, touching walls and bed and chest, and not bump into any other person. What luxury! I think if I were a king I would keep one room in my palace just for me, where I could go and be alone.

16TH DAY OF APRIL, *Feast of Saint Magnus, former Viking pirate*

Today my family met the villagers in a mock battle on the fishpond. All of the rickety handmade wooden boats sank but the sun was out and no one drowned. There are woolen kirtles and tunics and leggings hung from every tree and bush in the village and draped over the ovens and the dovecote here in the manor yard, while their owners run around near naked and white as plucked chickens, praying that the sun stay out until their finery is dry.

I cannot enjoy this week of Easter feasting. I am

too distracted by the Shaggy Beard matter. Lent is over and I have no plan.

17TH DAY OF APRIL, *Feast of Saint Donan and his fifty-two companions, killed by Vikings*

A messenger arrived this noon from Shaggy Beard. He is closeted with my father negotiating my sale. Until Morwenna found me and pulled me by my ear to the weaving loom, I listened to them argue. It was somewhat like this.

First, feet shuffling on the dry rushes. Then sword-rattling and throat-clearing. Finally an unfamiliar squeaky voice began: "Great Lord Murgaw of Lithgow, the Baron Selkirk, Lord of Smithburn, Random, and Fleece, brings greetings to Rollo of Stonebridge and announces his desire to honor Lord Rollo by an association with his daughter, the lady Catherine."

"On the contrary," my father replied, his voice low and as oily as buttered haddock. "My daughter, the lady Catherine, my pride and my joy, will honor the man she weds, not the other way round."

"Of course, Lord Rollo. Acknowledging that, the great Lord Murgaw, the Baron Selkirk, Lord of Lithgow, Smithburn, Random, and Fleece, put aside reasonable demands and bade me ask for dowry only your wife's manor of Greenwood, which lies next his own, four hundred silver coins, six oxen . . ." God's thumbs, I think myself worth at least seven oxen!

My father bellowed (I'll wager he turned purple),

"Dowry! He wants a dowry of me? Pay the pig to wed my jewel, my treasure, my angel, my only daughter? Out, sir! Away, sir! No more, sir!"

Aha, I thought. At last! I am delivered from the beast and the marriage by my father's greed. Another suitor gone. But then the messenger continued.

"Lord Rollo, understanding your tender love and care for the girl, the great lord Murgaw is willing to take but four oxen . . ."

Here Morwenna found me. I do not know if the messenger has been thrown out, if my father has choked from all the lies he tells, if Shaggy Beard is so determined to have me he will forego the oxen. But it matters not, for I still refuse to consider this marriage and will ignore the whole thing and hope the pig will die or fall in love with someone else or grow tired of my indifference.

18TH DAY OF APRIL, *Feast of Saint Laserian, an Irish monk who was struck with thirty diseases at once as penance for his sins*

The negotiations continue. From what I could overhear, the oxen are out and woven cloth is in. I am not consulted and no one has noticed that I am ignoring it all.

19TH DAY OF APRIL, *Feast of Saint Alphege, archbishop of Canterbury, killed by Vikings with the bones of an ox*

More talking. You would think my father and the agent of the loathsome Shaggy Beard were making peace with the Turks or preparing to invade France instead of arranging one little marriage.

In the midst of all the talking, my uncle George arrived for a visit, bringing his new wife, my aunt Ethelfritha. She is as mazed and crackled as an old mixing bowl. Wearing her grandfather's straw hat and her skirts tucked up into her belt, she sits at George's table, rides by his side, and sleeps in his bed. My guts are much troubled.

If not for my guts, I think I could love her. She fills our house, laughing louder than George, drinking more than my father, cooking better than our cook, and even ordering Morwenna about. She sheds tears over every lovely, sad, happy, or holy thing in the world and will eat no meat or fish or fowl for fear of causing pain to the creatures. Her dead husband, she says, still advises her—tells her where she left her straw hat or when to buy turnips. I would like to be like her when I am old.

20TH DAY OF APRIL, *Feast of Saint Caedwalla, king of Wessex, who was baptized a Christian and immediately died*

George told me of two cats who fought so fiercely that they ate each other up until nothing remained but their tails. I am pleased that he can still tease me, for else he seems much changed, slow and somber and silent. After supper I watched him doze by the fire, cradling one of the dogs Aelis brought to us long ago. I find I do not care for spells and meddling and being responsible for changing people's lives. I am going to bed.

21ST DAY OF APRIL, *Feast of Saint Maelrubba, apostle to the Picts*

I watched the villagers sowing the fields this morning. They looked like dancers, swaying side to side as they cast the seed left and right, followed by boys throwing rocks and sticks at the birds. In my head I understand the need to chase the birds away lest they eat all the seed and we have no oats or barley this year, but in my heart I weep for the hungry birds, and for a while I threw rocks and sticks at the boys.

Marriage talks continue. What do they have to talk about? I will not marry him, so it all means nothing.

22ND DAY OF APRIL, *Feast of Saint Theodore of Sykeon, who lived in an iron cage and made friends with wolves and bears*

My aunt Ethelfritha is behaving oddly. George says once long ago she was struck by lightning, which left her hair grizzled and her wits addled. Yestereve she sat at my mother's feet, strumming an imaginary lute and singing songs in make-believe Spanish. Today she thinks she is a sausage.

I was greatly worried for her but George said, "Let her go. She always comes back."

I am greatly worried for George, too. He is turning

into a guzzle-guts, drinking and scowling and using up all of my headache remedies. I am to blame for this. Remorse is eating my innards. If only he would smile again.

23RD DAY OF APRIL, *Feast of Saint George, slayer of dragons, and my uncle George's saint's day*

This morning Aelis came to see George on his saint's day but he would not. He drooped and sighed about the yard, heedlessly throwing rotted apples at the pigeons. A wretched Aelis wept noisily all over my chamber. I was overcome with bitter guilt and had to doctor myself with clary wine and custard to lift my spirits.

It did little good, for my turmoiling guts caused me to fight with my father about Shaggy Beard, with my mother about my father, and with Morwenna about everything. Normally I would talk to Aelis or George and feel better but they are too troubled to help me. I tried talking to Odd William who said, "In the illimitable sweep of time, what will it signify? What will you signify? What will any of us . . ." God's thumbs. I heaved a jug at him and fled the hall.

24TH DAY OF APRIL, *Feast of Saint Ives of Saint Ives, from whose buried body a miraculous spring flows*

Geoffrey has been called away from here. His father found a more important place for him to foster. I rejoice to see him go but still think sometimes on his golden hair and his lower lip.

25TH DAY OF APRIL, *Feast of Saint Mark, writer of gospels, whose bones lie in Venice*

I saw Shaggy Beard's messengers in the yard, talking solemnly to each other. Were the negotiations not going well? I decided to use my wiles to help drive them away. Finally I had something to do besides worry and wait.

I blackened my hair and teeth and acted like a fool, which worked once before, and for good measure let them hear me muttering to myself about meeting Gerd the miller's son in the barn. They looked at me with astonishment as I passed. Now, let it be over.

26TH DAY OF APRIL, *Feast of Saint Cletus, third pope*

Shaggy Beard's messengers left before dawn this day. No one will speak to me of what happened. Is it over? Am I delivered?

27TH DAY OF APRIL, *Feast of Saint Zita, a serving maid who would pray in ecstasy while angels did her chores*

I tried to talk to my father. He would not. When I pulled his sleeve, he cracked me and shouted, "Have off!" I think it is over. I have won. *Deo gratias.*

28TH DAY OF APRIL, *Feast of Saint Vitalis, martyred in Rome with his slave Agricola*

My father suffering from a sore throat, I made

him a gargle of strawberries, water, vinegar, and the dung of a white dog. Because of how hard he cracked me yesterday, I put in extra dung.

29TH DAY OF APRIL, *Feast of Saint Endellion, who lived on the milk of one cow*

We had a peddler in the yard this day. He brought hats, ribbons, gloves, pots, and other treasures to trade for goose quills, beeswax, and salt. My mother sent me to buy ribbons for her and I saw, hanging from the timbers of his cart, small cages of wicker woven like tiny castles with towers and gates. I had to have some for my birds, so I ran to my chamber to see what I might have to trade. I have no silks or velvets or laces and can't imagine anyone wanting my embroidery. Finally I rummaged through the rushes on the hall floor and found amidst the bones and grease drippings a penny and two farthings. The peddler had gone but I chased him down the road and traded the coins for three cages, which I have suspended from my ceiling beams with lavender ribbons. My chamber looks more and more like Heaven, let others who sleep there complain as they will.

30TH DAY OF APRIL, *May Day Eve and Feast of Saint Erkenwald, bishop of London*

The village is bustling as all prepare to go a-Maying tomorrow at dawn. My mother insists that Morwenna go with me, but I can easily avoid the old baggage if she spoils my fun.

I left open the window shutters in my chamber tonight so I could see the fires lit on every hill. I believe they are shining for me, for a future without Shaggy Beard. I am filled with hope.

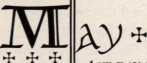

May ✠

1ST DAY OF MAY, *May Day and the Feast of Saint Marcoul, who cures corrupt and rotten ulcers, suppurating rashes, and other foul diseases of the skin*

The loveliest day of the year. To the Maypole haste away, for it is a holiday!

Morwenna and I went out before dawn to gather hawthorn and rowan branches alive with flowers and wash our faces in the magical May morn dew, though I think it is too late to improve Morwenna's face.

Gerd the miller's son and Ralph Littlemouse brought down from the hills a small birch, which we stripped of leaves and branches and decked with flowers and ribbons. We leapt and danced around it, singing in our glee to have summer come again. John Swann from the alehouse and William Steward's red-haired daughter Molly were acclaimed king and queen of the May. John Swann also won most of the games, the wrestling and the running and the stick fighting, although Perkin climbed highest in the old oak. The village boys spent their time trying to kiss the queen and any other girl they could reach.

We feasted on berries and bread and cakes and ale in the orchard, and near noon Jack o' the Green came dancing in, his face and body covered with leaves, singing about maidens and love and kissing. I tied leaves and flowers about myself and danced with Jack and then John Swann and then John Swann again. Molly pulled him off to dance with her, and I tried to dance off with Jack as he left the village, but Morwenna stopped me, as I hoped she would.

2ND DAY OF MAY, *Feast of Saint Gennys, not the one who carried his own head*

I am confounded. Shaggy Beard's agents, gone these last days, have come again. Shaggy Beard, it seems, is determined, and my behavior and my wishes affect him not at all. Is he the suitor more greedy than my father and more stubborn than I? Oh, God, I pray not.

The messengers' return changes nothing. *I will not marry the pig!*

A wonder: I have not the powers to avoid Shaggy Beard. Did I then truly have anything to do with George and Aelis? Or was there no curse?

3RD DAY OF MAY, *Feast of the Finding of the Holy Cross*

May Perkin roast in Hell. I asked him this

morning for a small kiss so I might know what all the fuss and poetry and song is about, but he just laughed and would not.

4TH DAY OF MAY, *Feast of Saint Monica, who overcame a violent husband and a tendency to heavy drinking to become mother of the holy Saint Augustine*

I put my shoes on the wrong feet this morning and it brought me ill luck indeed, for the negotiations are over and I am set to marry Shaggy Beard. My mother asked that I not be wed and gone until her baby is born in the autumn, so I have a morsel of time left to figure a way out of this trouble. If only I had been able to become a monk or a crusader or a pilgrim or anything but a maid about to be sold like a herring. I am sulking and have refused all food since dinner.

5TH DAY OF MAY, *Feast of Saint Hydroc of Lanhydroc, a Cornish hermit*

Fought with the beast my father over this joke of a marriage. I roared, he roared, I threw things, he stepped on them, I pushed him, he shouted about stubbornness and pride which should long ago have been broken and delivered several hard blows to my face.

6TH DAY OF MAY, *Feast of Saints Marian and James, blindfolded, beheaded, and thrown into the river Rummel*

Fought again with my father. God gave me this big mouth, so I think it can be no sin to use it. Even so, I plan to resume sulking instead of arguing—it is much easier on my face.

7TH DAY OF MAY, *Feast of Saint Stanislaus of Poland, killed by some king while he prayed*

Still sulking and have added deep sighs and ill temper. My father looks about to burst with anger. Good.

I spent the afternoon in the far field with Perkin and the goats. He said my father manages me all wrong. Perkin said he learned about getting along with me by watching Sym with the pigs. If it is necessary to lead a pig forward, he said, Sym ties a string to its hind leg and pulls backward. The pig will then pull forward and so goes ahead. And so it is with me, Perkin says. If my father pulled me backward, I would demand to go ahead.

I mislike being likened to a pig, so left Perkin in the field and am sulking in the barn—alone.

8TH DAY OF MAY, *Feast of Saint Indract, an Irish prince who with his nine traveling companions was set upon and murdered by brigands*

More lady-lessons. It is impossible to do all and be all a lady must be and not tie oneself in a knot. A lady must walk erect with dignity, looking straight before her with eyelids low, gazing at the ground ahead, neither trotting nor running nor looking about nor laughing nor stopping to chatter. Her hands must be folded below her cloak while at the same time lifting her dress from the floor while at the same time hiding her mouth if her smile is unattractive or her teeth yellow. A lady must have six hands!

She must not look too proud nor yet too humble, lest people say she is proud of her humility. She must not talk overmuch yet not be silent, lest people think she does not know how to converse. She must not show anger, nor sulk, nor scold, nor overeat, nor over-drink, nor swear. God's thumbs! I am going out to the barn to jump, fart, and pick my teeth!

9TH DAY OF MAY, *Feast of Saint Beatus of Vendome, who lived and died in a cave, where he fought and slew a dragon*

More arguing with my father and more bruises. As Morwenna bathed my face in rosemary water she said, "Child, a dog is wiser than you. He does not bark at his own master."

Perkin likens me to a pig, Morwenna to a dog. I wish I were one or the other.

10TH DAY OF MAY, *Feast of Saint Conleth, who was de-voured by wolves*

My mother still troubled by headache, I made her a tonic of chamomile, being out of goat dung until Perkin brings the goats home. No relief.

11TH DAY OF MAY, *Feast of Saint Credan, who killed his father and in remorse became a hogherd and a saint*

I wonder how he did it.

14TH DAY OF MAY, *Feast of Saint Boniface, who led a dissipated life but was kind to the poor and died while protecting Christians*

My mother being ill these past days, I have had no time for writing or, in truth, anything to write.

15TH DAY OF MAY, *Feast of Saint Dympna, protector of lunatics*

We sent for the Spanish physician who is visiting the abbey to see to my mother's headaches, for Morwenna and I can do no more. He is a little man in a black cape and a flat black hat that looks very like a big burned pancake. He advised her to avoid bad smells, keep her head cool, and not to cry, sing high, or shout hallo. I advised her to get rid of the Spanish physician.

17TH DAY OF MAY, *Feast of Saint Madron of Cornwall, whose magic well one can still visit*

My mother does better, I am still promised to Shaggy Beard, it is raining. Life goes on.

18TH DAY OF MAY, *Feast of Saint Aelgifu, queen of Wessex, mother of Kings Edwy and Edgar*

I think Aelgifu a more suiting name for me than Catherine or Birdy. I asked Morwenna henceforth to call me Aelgifu but she merely snorted.

19TH DAY OF MAY, *Feast of Saint Dunstan, who pinched the Devil's nose with tongs*

Still raining. I sat in the hall with Odd William, who also refuses to call me Aelgifu but did read to me from his history of the world. He has just finished writing of the Trojan War and of Aeneas, who fled to Italy from the ruins of Troy, and his grandson Brutus, who was expelled from Italy for shooting his father with an arrow, thinking him an animal, although it seems to me a reasonable mistake. After many adventures this Brutus came to the island of Albion, inhabited only by giants, and he and his followers built homes and settled down to stay, changing the name of the island to Britain, after Brutus. I asked Odd William why in that case it was not Brutain. He humphed and stopped reading and I had to leave the comfort of the hall and find a place to hide from Morwenna and her everlasting weaving.

20TH DAY OF MAY, *Feast of Saint Ethelbert, king of East Anglia, a relative, no doubt, of my aunt Ethelfritha*
Still raining. No one will agree to call me Aelgifu except Gerd the miller's son, who cannot pronounce the name and says Ugly-foo.

21ST DAY OF MAY, *Feast of Saint Collen, a Welshman who fought a duel with a Saracen before the pope, went home to Wales, and delivered the people in the Vale of Llangollen from a lady giant by slaying her*
I asked Odd William about this story of Saint Collen, for it seems the sort of thing he would know.

William says it is but a fable, that Saint Collen did indeed fight a Saracen and a lady giant but the pope was never involved.

How pleasant it has been to lie by the fire and hear stories and think about Greeks and giants and popes. Mayhap I could be William's apprentice.

22ND DAY OF MAY, *Feast of Saint Helen of Carnavon, builder of Welsh roads*

In order to put an end to my idleness, which Morwenna says is the great pathway that leads to all evils, I have been made to hem sheets for my marriage bed. By cock and pie! Would that I had thread spun from deadly henbane or spurge!

This sewing of sheets makes a marriage seem more real. What am I to do? Am I doomed?

25TH DAY OF MAY, *Feast of Saint Zenobius of Florence who raised from the dead five people including a child run over by an ale cart in front of the cathedral*

Grown full restless with the rain, I thought to sing some of my songs to Odd William. He is after all a great scholar and could give me an opinion of them. I had just begun my Lenten song when he commenced talking of his own work and the difficulty of obtaining enough paper and how he is contemplating next a life of Merlin the Magician in rhymed couplets. He did not see me or hear me at all. Finally I wandered off to throw gooseberries into the fire. They popped and hissed—made as much sense as Odd William. He will have to find another apprentice.

28TH DAY OF MAY, *Feast of Saint Bernard of Aosta, who used dogs to help lost travelers on the Alpine passes*

Walter Grey, the steward of Crossbridge Manor, stopped here today to drink our ale and to boast of a miracle in Crossbridge village. One of the villagers, he says, an unlettered man with no language but English, woke up one morning suddenly able to speak fluent Hebrew. We once had a two-headed calf, which I think much superior to Hebrew-speaking villagers, but it didn't live very long.

29TH DAY OF MAY, *Feast of Saint Alexander, martyred in Milan*

The news of the Hebrew-speaking villager has greatly excited Odd William. This, if true, he says, supports his growing suspicion that Brutus and the early Britons were not Trojans but members of one of the lost tribes of Israel, driven from their homeland by the Assyrians. A villager who miraculously remembers Hebrew from the Britons' long-ago past would confirm his theory.

William plans to ride to Crossbridge to see for himself. He has visions of glory and renown, with famed scholars coming from all over the world to consult him. Probably they will all want to sleep in my chamber.

30TH DAY OF MAY, *Feast of Saint Hubert, who became a Christian when he saw the image of the crucified Christ between the antlers of a stag*

There was a wondrous strange spectacle in our yard this dawn. Odd William tied his writing table, parchments, and pens onto the back of the miller's mule and set out for Crossbridge and fame. His eyes, so well suited for close work like writing, fail at distances, so that William rides leaning greatly forward on the mule's neck, alternately squinting and peering far ahead, while rubbing that spot between his eyes where all this squinting and peering hurts him. Our villagers lined the road and called out to him as he passed, thinking him some sort of saint or holy man for his part in the Crossbridge miracle. Dogs, two goats, a goose, and several village children ran behind him, spattered with the drops the ink made as it spilled its way to Crossbridge. I should like to paint a picture of this on my chamber wall, but I fear I would never then sleep for laughing.

31ST DAY OF MAY, *Feast of Saint Petronilla, who refused to marry a pagan count and starved herself to death*

The rain has stopped and the world shines. Everything seems more hopeful in the sun. It will soon be summer and I am not Lady Shaggy Beard yet. I *will* find a way out.

June

1ST DAY OF JUNE *Feast of Saint Gwen of Brittany, who had three breasts*

Odd William has returned. He says the miraculous Hebrew the villager spoke was but gibberish, the product of a brain fever or an overactive imagination. Gone are William's hopes for greatness. He is standing again, his back to our fire, writing of the founding of Rome by twin orphans nursed by a wolf.

2ND DAY OF JUNE, *Feast of Saints Marcellinus and Peter, Christian martyrs, who converted their jailor while in prison*

There was a message from Robert. His wife has died with as little fuss as she lived. I never once called her by name. It was Agnes. The child died too. It had no name.

Strange things are happening to me. I am having so many soft feelings. Mayhap I need to brew me some wormwood and periwinkle, to comfort my heart.

3RD DAY OF JUNE *Whitsunday and the Feast of Saint Kevin, who lived on salmon brought to him by an otter and died at one hundred twenty*

We dressed all in green and yellow to celebrate Whit Day and sang "Summer is icumen in," although it was so cold and rainy that the dancers fought to wear the tree costumes, which are clumsy but warm, and all were wet and bedraggled. We were happy to think on the church ale to come.

4TH DAY OF JUNE, *Feast of Saint Edfrith, scribe and artist, like me*

Quiet today. I am sore of head and sour of stomach but warm.

5TH DAY OF JUNE, *Feast of Saint Boniface, who wrote the first Latin grammar used in England*

I helped an ant today. She carried a burden so heavy it looked to crush her. A crumb it was, or a speck of wheat. Or a drop of honey that had hardened in the sun. She was struggling to take it back to her nest, where it would feed her fellow ants for a day or a week, as small as it was. So intent was she on carrying her crumb that she didn't notice me at all. I watched as she staggered and fell and bumped and stumbled, making slow progress toward what must have been her home.

But day was nearly over. I knew the villagers would be driving their animals back through the meadow to pen them for the night. And the tiny ant and her precious crumb would be smashed into the dirt. I had to help her.

First I searched around for other ants, to see where they were going. I followed a line of ants running to and from a hole in the dirt, some in, some out, some sideways, all around the hole. This must be home, I thought.

I put a piece of a leaf in front of the ant. All intent on her burden and unaware of me, she walked onto the leaf. Then I went to the hole in the dirt where all the ant activity was. It was only a few steps for me but seemed a lifetime's journey for an ant. I put the leaf down by the hole. The ant walked around the leaf, up the stem and down the side, stumbled around in circles for a bit, twitched her feelers like my brother Robert hitching up his breeches, and walked down the ant hole, still balancing her morsel. I felt as though I had saved the whole world.

6TH DAY OF JUNE *Feast of Saints Gudwal, Jarlath, Norbert, Agabard, Artemius, Candida, and Pauline. Truly, I am not making this up*

The beast my father woke up roaring like a real beast this morning. Toothache. He rubbed garlic on his thumb and left the smelly paste there all day, but that reliable remedy failed him. He roars that he will go to Lincoln to the tooth puller, but my mother is afraid that pulling the tooth will leave a hole in his head where evil spirits can get into his body. I think it more likely that evil spirits could get out.

8TH DAY OF JUNE *Feast of Saint William of York, at whom my great-great-great-great-grandmother once threw a cabbage*

My mother convinced the beast to send to the abbey for the Spanish physician. She thinks mayhap he can cure my father's toothache without leaving a hole.

11TH DAY OF JUNE *Feast of Saint Barnabas, the first missionary*

Two days ago the Spanish physician was here. He told my father that the toothache is due to an imbalance of humors in his body and recommended letting out some excess blood by cutting a vein under his tongue. The beast submitted meekly—or him—until the knife pierced his tongue. He swung out and knocked the little man from Spain from his stool. Finally the physician managed to cut the vein and caught the heavy dark blood in a cooking pot.

But today the beast still roared, so the physician returned. The toothache, it seems, comes not from unbalanced humors but from a toothworm, which has burrowed deep into my father's jaw. This new cause required a new remedy so the physician mixed henbane leaves with sheep fat, rolled this into little pellets, and dropped them on the fire. My father leaned over and breathed in the smoke through his mouth. Sparks kept leaping up and starting his beard on fire—he looked like a demon from the mouth of Hell, smoldering and bellowing. I went outside and helped Meg make cheese.

13TH DAY OF JUNE, *Feast of Saint Antony of Padua, who once preached to fish*

We go today to Lincoln to the tooth puller! The physician came again yesterday, escorted by six of my father's men. He told my father that this tooth-worm was especially stubborn and malignant and that nothing would do but a poultice of raven manure on the sore tooth. I saw the little man running, robes pulled up over hairy skinny legs, followed by my father's roar, and not even his six escorts could bring him back.

Morwenna convinced my mother that we need new embroidery silks that none but she and I could select, so we go too! It is Corpus Christi week and on Thursday the guilds of Lincoln will deck their wagons with flowers and herbs and pull them through the town to the cathedral square, where they will perform their plays about the wonders of Creation and the life of Jesus and I will be there to see! God keep Morwenna!

19TH DAY OF JUNE, *Feast of Saints Gervase and Protase, whose relics restored the sight of a blind butcher in Milan*

Corpus bones! Since last I wrote I have seen Heaven and Hell, angels and devils, and the tortures of the damned. I must be much changed.

We rode to Lincoln in a fine drizzle, but the city atop its hill was bathed in sunshine. From our room in the inn I could hear the sharp cracking of horses' hooves on cobblestone, the cries of merchants and peddlers, the cook boys calling "Hot pies! Fat pigs and geese! Come and eat!" and the incredible noise of too many people in too small a space.

Lincoln is wondrous fair and curious. On our way to the tooth puller we walked streets so steep a fat bishop pushed from the top would not stop rolling until he reached the river Trent. On either side were merchants' booths with wares spread out upon the counters—cloth, ribbons, candles, needles, boots, belts, spoons, knives, arrowheads, and more. Above the shops the second stories leaned so far over the street that Mistress A could pass a sausage to Mistress B across the road without leaving her house.

The crowded city swarmed with dogs, cats, roosters, geese, pigs, horses, merchants, travelers, housewives hurrying to market, children running with their buckets to the well, serving maids emptying chamber pots, and all manner of busy, bustling creatures. Near the market square we passed a man with his head and hands held tight in stocks, being pulled through the streets in a wagon. Caught selling spoiled fish, he had some of his stinking goods hung round his neck like a necklace, and the wagon was followed by hundreds of cats, hungry and hoping. Children and even some vengeful housewives followed along, throwing sticks and mud and garbage at the wagon. One old woman threw rotten carrots and onions while another gathered them up in her apron and hurried off to make soup.

When we reached the tooth puller the beast roared again, but the tooth is now out. His jaw is black and swollen—I thought perhaps my mother was right and evil spirits had entered, but he roars no louder and swears no more and stinks no worse, so mayhap all is well.

The next day being Corpus Christi, we heard Mass and then followed a procession of priests and merchants into the cathedral yard to see them play the story of the Last Judgment. A two-tiered wagon held Heaven on its upper story and Earth below. At the side was the mouth of Hell, smoke and flames belching out, and the awful cries of the damned, suffering every kind of beating, roasting, and grilling. I hope to have nightmares from this for months!

Heaven was remarkably crowded, considering how few people we are told are good enough to get there. Angels with golden skin and golden wings flew about on golden straps, playing on golden harps. One angel caught on the branches of an apple tree. The angel struggled and cursed devilish curses but finally climbed down unhurt, and the play went on, with God and the saints singing and dancing and blowing on golden horns, calling each man to answer for his deeds.

Below on Earth, demons bristling with horned horsehair masks tried to drag sinners into the mouth of Hell, while behind their backs the Virgin Mary pulled the poor souls out of the hellfire with her own hands. Then the Devil himself appeared, hoofed, horned, and tailed, clad in a wolf skin, bedecked in bells, shaggy and awful and smelling like last week's herring. In a deep ringing voice he called, "Foul-tempered wives, who cause men to grieve, murderers, thieves, my welcome receive!"

If he had called for disobedient daughters, I think I would have repented my sins and cried for mercy right there in the cathedral yard!

One clumsy devil knocked over the ladder to Heaven, smashing it to bits and stranding players up above. While someone built another, God and the angels entertained us with songs and bawdy stories. Then the new ladder went up, we all cheered, God came down waving to the audience, and the play was over.

20TH DAY OF JUNE, *Feast of Saint Alban, beheaded by a soldier whose eyes then fell out. Saint Alban is buried near here. At Saint Alban's*

We returned in the midst of furious housecleaning. The courtyard and the orchard were bedecked with wet linen, hanging from ropes and walls and trees, while kettles bubbled with strong-smelling soapy water. Tonight my body will rejoice—clean linen!

Home can never match the excitement of Lincoln, but I was happy to see my mother again. She is well and the babe she carries too, God save us all.

21ST DAY OF JUNE, *Feast of Saint Leufred, forty-eight years an abbot*

Old Tam, the father of Meg from the dairy, finally has three pigs, so Meg will marry Thomas Baker's oldest son, Alf, as soon as they have a cottage. Alf is puny and sneezes all summer, but still I would be Meg, about to marry the choice of my heart, rather than the lady Catherine, promised to a pig. I am desolate.

22ND DAY OF JUNE, *Feast of Saint Ebbe the Younger, who cut off her nose to protect her virtue from marauding Danes*

This afternoon was flea-catching. I spread a white cloth on each bed so even my weak eyes could see the little black fleas as they jumped. I then caught each one and crushed it between my finger and thumb. It is tedious and leaves me bumpy and red with bites, but does not overvex my brain, so I can think and wonder while I work.

Today I thought about ways the shaggy-bearded oaf who wishes to marry me might die and leave me free. He might be eaten by wolves or struck by lightning or explode from eating too much. He might encounter a dragon bigger and meaner and more evil even than he or be disemboweled by a

Turk or a jealous husband. Mayhap all his teeth will fall out and he will be unable to eat and so will starve to death. Or he might jump off a roof in a drunk, thinking he could fly. He could be run over by a peddler's wagon full of heavy iron pots or have corrupt and rotten ulcers eat away his body. I could put deadly thorn apple or monkshood in his soup or train my birds to fly north and peck him to death. Or a giant hand might reach down and pinch him between its thumb and finger. Life is full of possibilities. If only something would happen soon.

23RD DAY OF JUNE *Midsummer Eve and Feast of Saint Ethelreda, who died of a tumor on her neck, divine punishment for her vanity in wearing necklaces in her younger days*

All of the world is celebrating Midsummer Eve, eating and drinking and dancing in the fields. I cannot, filled as I am with dread over this marriage business. If only the bonfires lit throughout the shire this night to drive demons and dragons away would drive unwelcome suitors away as well. I am going to bed with the sounds of singing in my ears but not in my heart.

24TH DAY OF JUNE, *Midsummer Day and Feast of Saint John the Baptist, Our Lord's cousin, whose head King Herod gave to Salome as a reward for her dancing*

Where will next Midsummer Day find me?

25TH DAY OF JUNE, *Feast of Adalbert of Egmond, about whom we know nothing but who works miracles at his tomb*

Last night Ralph Littlemouse dreamed he saw Perkin's granny sitting by the side of the road with blood on her clothes.

This morning he ran to her cottage but she was already dead. He thinks she must have been elf-shot, for there are no marks on her, so we all are carrying bread in our pockets to protect us from the fairies.

Glynna Cotter and Thomas Baker's wife, Ann, washed and dressed the old woman and laid her on the table in her cottage. Tonight all the villagers will watch. I do not know why they call it watching when it is really singing and games and drinking, but at least she will not be alone.

They have sent to the high meadow for Perkin to come home. My heart breaks for him.

26TH DAY OF JUNE, *Feast of John and Paul, Roman martyrs, who were buried in their garden*

We took Perkin's granny from her cottage to the church in the dark, although I could see a sliver of silver light to the east and knew dawn would soon be upon us.

Father Huw said Mass and a lot of things about sinners and hellfire and how this should be a mirror to us all for we all shall die and none know when—but nothing about how she had the merriest eyes I ever saw. Or how although she was no bigger than Ralph Littlemouse's youngest, she always had a lap big enough for a crying child. Or how she made the best soul cakes in the village.

I tried to convince Perkin to sleep in our hall tonight but he said no, he will spread his bed by the fire in his granny's cottage as he always does when he is not in the high meadow with the goats, and will do so every night until he leaves to be a scholar.

27TH DAY OF JUNE, *Feast of Saint Cyril of Alexandria, fierce enemy of the Novatians, Neoplatonists, Nestorians, and the imperial governor Orestes*

Before light this day I awoke with an inspired notion. I slipped out of my bed and into my clothes and was at the dairy before light. Meg was already there, trying to coax milk from an unwilling cow.

"Meg, I have an inspired notion," I said. "You and Alf need a cottage. Perkin's granny does not. I think God sent Perkin's granny's cottage to you."

Meg's eyes lit as though I had set a torch light to them. "A cottage," she sighed. "Married," she sighed. "Me and Alf," she sighed.

We jumped around the dairy a bit and then Meg stopped, biting her lip and scowling. "Your father, my lady. Would he? Could we? Could you?"

I knew what she was trying to ask. While Meg finished coaxing the cows, I went to coax my father.

I found him in the hall with his breakfast bread

and ale, frowning at the snoring lump that was Odd William, lying between himself and the warmth of the fire.

"Sir," said I. "The morning dawns fair. I hope it finds you well."

"Slurp," said my father.

"For certain," I continued, "Perkin's granny is in Heaven this day, watching over us all. I know God would want her with Him, so good she was, and so generous. God ever rewards the generous."

"Slurp," said my father again.

"Generous as she was, I know Perkin's granny would want to share what she had with those of us left behind. Her warmest mantle with the miller's wife, her extra stockings with Ann Baker. And," I said, taking a big breath, "her empty cottage with young about-to-weds who have none of their own."

My father stopped in mid-slurp. His brain woke up. He understood. Greed blossomed in his tiny eyes, and he bargained with me for the cottage. Finally he agreed to let Meg and Alf have it in exchange for one of Meg's dowry pigs and my willingness to consider the Shaggy Beard marriage.

So I told Meg, and Meg told Alf, and they will be married on Sunday and have Perkin's granny's cottage. Perkin will still have his bed by the fire when he is not in the high meadow with the goats, and someone to see he eats a hot meal on cold days. And his granny in Heaven will smile at me and all will be well.

28TH DAY OF JUNE, *Saint Peter's Eve and Feast of the martyrs Saint Potamiaena, who had boiling pitch poured over her body, and Saint Basilides, a soldier who was kind to her*

I had good reason to hide from Morwenna today, for I had the notion to make a picture for Perkin of his granny in Heaven and did not wish to be stopped and made to sew or weave or practice walking with my eyes down. I used my best inks and brushes and a new whole sheet of vellum taken by night from the stack William Steward uses for the household accounts. In my picture the sun shines, for Perkin's granny suffered greatly from the cold. She is gaily dressed in a new green kirtle and dances in a meadow with Perkin and goats, for I think Heaven would be no Heaven for either of them without goats. She is smiling and has all her teeth.

Perkin leaves in two days to return to the high meadow, so I will leave the picture in the cottage where he will be sure to find it.

30TH DAY OF JUNE, *Feast of Saint Theobald of Provins, hermit, patron of charcoal burners*

Perkin has gone, but first brought to me his thanks, his granny's earthenware cup, and a kiss. My insides are very warm although the morning is cool.

July

1ST DAY OF JULY, *Feast of Saints Julius and Aaron, British farmers, who suffered horrible physical tortures at the hands of the Romans*

I was at Meg's father's cottage before light this day to bring her the gift of my second-best blue kirtle, her only one being old and patched and green, a color sure to bring bad luck to a bride. I then went to the church to await everyone at the church door, where William Steward and I would represent my father on this occasion. Meg said it would bring them great honor and great luck. I think the luck is that my father did not come himself.

Soon I heard the sound of laughter and singing and the strumming of gitterns as Meg and Alf led the villagers up the path to the church. Meg's yellow hair, usually tightly plaited and pinned up so as not to hang in the milk or become tangled in the butter churn, fell loose in a river of gold to her knees. A circlet of bluebells and cowslips and day's eyes crowned her shining head. My blue kirtle matched her eyes. Morwenna says beauty and rainbows soon pass away, but I know for the rest of my life when I look at Meg I will see her like this.

Alf looked much the same as always except he had no flour in his hair.

After exchanging vows at the church door, Alf gave Meg half a penny and kept the other half for himself so that, he said, they would always remember they were two halves of one soul. It was very pretty. Then Mass and, with church bells ringing, to the alehouse for the bride ale. Since the sky was the same clear blue as Meg's eyes, John Swann had set up tables outside, strewn with rosemary, bay, and the petals of the wild white rose.

The afternoon was gay with music and dancing and much ale-drinking, with the pennies paid for the ale to go to Meg for her new cottage.

Now it grows dark and I am in my chamber writing. The party continues and will all night—some will even have bride ale for breakfast—but Meg and Alf have gone home to the cottage God sent them, with help from Perkin's granny and me.

2ND DAY OF JULY, *Feast of Saints Processus and Martinian, Roman martyrs, whose relics cure the sick, reveal perjurers, and cure lunatics*

I have been thinking about my own marriage.

Once I dreamed of a handsome prince on a white horse decked in silks and bells. Now I am offered a smelly, broken-toothed old man who drinks too much. I would rather even Alf! But it occurred to me that what actually makes people married is not the church or the priest but their consent, their "I will." And I do not consent. Will never consent. "I will not." I cannot be wed without my consent, can I? They cannot bind me with ropes and force my mouth open and closed while my father says in a high voice, "I will." I am told this has happened, but even my father could not be so cruel. I will not consent and there will be no marriage. Amen.

4TH DAY OF JULY *Feast of Saint Andrew of Crete, stabbed to death by a fanatical Iconoclast*

I spent this summer evening lying in the field, watching stars come out in the sky. Free. Free. Free! After my harrowing days locked away, I rejoice to be free. It was like this:

The evening after Meg's wedding, I encountered my father near the buttery.

"Now we will get on with it, daughter," he said. "It is time to make good your promise and consent to marriage with Murgaw."

"Never," I said. "Your villagers are allowed to marry where they will, but your daughter is sold like a cheese for your profit! Never."

He blinked three times, opening and closing his mouth. Then his face grew purple and he choked out disconnected words: "Meg . . . cottage . . . promise . . . marriage."

"I promised to consider such a marriage, sir, and I did, I said. "I considered it and I reject it. I will not consent."

So there was shouting and slapping and stomping away, which ended with me locked in my prison of a chamber without my inks in an attempt to break my spirit.

Earlier this evening he came to my chamber, the only person I had seen in two days except Morwenna and Wat.

Standing in the doorway, he said, "Your mother has prevailed upon me to let you out. You are to go down to supper. You will be quiet, agreeable, and obedient. And you will wed the pig."

He left the door open. I am free. And I will *not* wed the pig.

5TH DAY OF JULY, *Feast of Saint Morwenna, an Irish maiden who worked miracles*

This morning I strewed the bed with flowers for my Morwenna, who irritates and torments me sometimes but whom I love. Hers is the first face I ever saw.

6TH DAY OF JULY, *Feast of Saint Sexburga, wife of Erconbert, mother of Erkengota and Ermengild*

Aelis's baby husband has died and she is a widow without ever really being a wife. Since she met him but seldom, I think mayhap she is none too sad. I wonder if George knows.

7TH DAY OF JULY, *Feast of Saint Willibald, who wrote a book called* Hodoeporicon *about his travels to Rome, Cyprus, Syria, and the Holy Land*

My father left this day for London. The manor is already quieter and cleaner, and I can breathe more easily.

8TH DAY OF JULY, *Feast of Saint Urith of Chittlehampton, killed by jealous haymakers*

After Mass this day I walked over to Perkin's granny's cottage, now home to Meg and Alf. Parsnips and mutton were boiling on a pot over the fire, making the July day inside the cottage much hotter than outside. The air was gray and smoky; the dirt floor was fresh swept but still dirt; the small straw bed, Perkin's mat on the floor, and the table where Perkin's granny served meals all her life and was laid out the day of her death were still the only furniture, but the small dark cottage seemed different, somehow lighter and smelling young rather than old. There was such a feeling of love in there, of Meg and Alf and their babies and their grandchildren to come, all together in this cottage, living their days together.

Meg offered me some of the parsnip and mutton but all sorts of sad and happy feelings were stuck in my throat like a lump and I knew I couldn't swallow. So I went home alone to the hall.

10TH DAY OF JULY, *Feast of the Seven Brothers of Rome, martyred with the encouragement of their mother, Saint Felicity, who was also martyred*

I am overhot and as limp as dirty linen. This heat promises a good harvest but sore distresses my mother. I sit each day with her, embroidering tiny clothes for the coming babe and telling stories to take her mind from her body. I fear for her.

12TH DAY OF JULY, *Feast of Saint Veronica, who wiped the face of the suffering Jesus with her veil, where His image remains to this day*

It is too hot to write. Too hot even for the cats to chase mice.

13TH DAY OF JULY, *Feast of Saint Mildred, who became a nun to escape the attentions of an unwelcome suitor. There* must *be a better way*

In this heat my mother suffers much from swelling of her legs, which means the baby likely will be a girl. I applied a paste of bean meal, flour, vinegar, and oil, but the dogs kept trying to eat it. So I washed her off and have been rubbing her legs with sweet-smelling oils and singing her sweet songs and it seems to help.

15TH DAY OF JULY, *Feast of Saint Swithin, who wept in Heaven and caused forty days of rain*

As I rubbed my mother's legs late into the night,

she talked again about her first meeting with my father. I am amazed how soft and sweet her voice grows when she speaks of that big, dirty, rude, greedy, drunken beast. I told her it is as if we see two different men. She said marriage can do that.

"Marriage," I said to her, "seems to me to be but spinning, bearing children, and weeping."

Smiling, she said, "Marriage is what you make it, Birdy. If you spit in the air, it will fall on your face. Patience, gentleness, and a willing heart will make the most of any union. It helps, of course," she added softly, "if the man you marry is the fine kind of figure that your father . . ."

God's thumbs, enough of this talk of my father's virtues. She must have caught warble fly from the cows and it has gone to her brain.

17TH DAY OF JULY, *Feast of Saint Alexis, who lived as a slave in his father's house and slept under the stairs*

I met Aelis this day in the meadow. She is giddy and relieved to be married no longer. She says when she married the baby duke, her father promised her that if she ever married again she would have more choice about the man. Now that the baby duke is dead and Aelis a widow, she is determined to love and be loved as well as wed. I know she is speaking about George, but I do not know what will come. My aunt Ethelfritha may be a bit mad but she is definitely alive.

18TH DAY OF JULY, *Feasts of Saints Edburga of Bicester and Edburga of Winchester but not Edburga of Minster*

The northern shaggy-bearded pig has sent me betrothal gifts, which I, of course, refused since I will not consent to marry him. He sent me a silver toothpick, a sewing kit, a gauze headdress in a stinking green that is my least becoming color, and a pouch of silver. Corpus bones! His gifts are as unromantic and as unwanted as he is.

His son Stephen sent me a bronze knife engraved on the blade with vines and leaves and the words "Think well on me," a most excellent gift.

20TH DAY OF JULY, *Feast of Saint Margaret of Antioch, eaten by a dragon who then exploded. Protector of women in childbirth*

O dear Saint Margaret, protect my mother when her time comes. She is old—over thirty—and delicate. But you were strong and stubborn and I can be as tough as boiled bear, so mayhap together we can sustain her.

21ST DAY OF JULY *Feast of Saint Victor, Roman soldier and martyr*

George and my aunt Ethelfritha have come again. He still does not smile and his eyes no longer flash green fire. He drinks too much ale and closes his eyes whenever someone mentions Aelis's name. I could feel his pain as if we shared one heart, so I left the table and went out to pester Perkin.

22ND DAY OF JULY *Feast of Saint Mary Magdalene, who was betrothed to John the Apostle*

Morwenna, Meg, and I have been gathering summer herbs and flowers for tonics. I love walking the fields in the morning sun, the smells in the stillroom where the herbs hang to dry, the wondrous glass vials and leather bottles arranged on the shelves, the old book where my mother's mother and her mother wrote recipes and hints and warnings for the doctoring.

Many of the older remedies call for lark's wing or boiled raven. I will not use them but use instead fish bones or nail trimmings or extra rue and sneezewort. No one here at the manor has died since I have been doing so and I expect my remedies doctor just as well as the originals. And they are much kinder to the birds.

24TH DAY OF JULY, *Feast of Saint Gleb, stabbed in the throat by his cook*

I have begun an herbal, a book of remedies and drawings that I can have with me always wherever I go.

26TH DAY OF JULY *Feast of Saint Ann, mother of the Virgin Mary*

I have noticed lately how many male saints were bishops, popes, missionaries, great scholars, and teachers, while female saints get to be saints mostly by being someone's mother or refusing to marry some powerful pagan. It is plain that men are in charge of making saints.

27TH DAY OF JULY, *Feast of the Seven Sleepers, early Christians who were walled up in a cave by pagans, awoke two hundred years later to find their entire city Christian, and died*

A traveler sleeping in our hall last night said Brother Norbert and Brother Behrtwald, the monks sent to Rome to find the remains of saints for our abbey, have returned. The holy relics they found will be installed with great ceremony in the abbey on Sunday. My father being from home and my mother too big with child for traveling, George, Ethelfritha, and I will appear for our family. I am rapturous with holy feelings to think I will see pieces of actual saints, whose souls must be with God although their bodies lie in Croydon Abbey.

We leave at dawn tomorrow.

28TH DAY OF JULY, *Feast of Saint Samson, Welsh bishop, whose arm and staff are at the monastery at Milton Abbas*

After dinner in the abbey guesthouse, I looked for Brother Norbert so I might hear more about the saints he found in Rome and his adventures on the way. Brother Norbert, I was told, was weeding the herb garden. Brother Norbert, I discovered, was sleeping between the lavender and rosemary bushes. I cleared my throat several times loudly and soon he awoke.

The relics the monks brought from Rome, it seems, are the earthly remains of Felix the Roman and his brother Projectus. They were tax collectors, converted to Christianity by a bath attendant and betrayed to the authorities by their evil servant, Polycarp, who was later struck by lightning.

Ordered to sacrifice to Roman gods, Felix and Projectus agreed, in fear for their lives and those of their families. A sudden rainstorm, however, put out the sacrificial fire. The Romans were enraged, thinking the brothers had lied to them and doused the fire deliberately by magic.

Their explanations were ignored and the brothers were condemned to be beheaded, but the soldier sent to carry out the sentence was struck by lightning. Finally they were set upon by a maddened bull, who, after goring them to death, was also struck by lightning. Other Christians collected their body parts and buried them on a farm outside the city.

This summer Brother Norbert and Brother Behrtwald met a soldier in an inn yard, who told them the story and then, for only twelve silver pennies, led them to the martyrs' grave on his mother's property. It was fortunate, said Brother Norbert, that they had the soldier to guide them, for the grave was hidden and unmarked in any way. The good brothers left Rome with the martyrs' bones, a fingernail clipping, and a thread from Felix's best tunic. Glory be to God.

29TH DAY OF JULY, *Feast of Saint Lupus, a bishop who persuaded Attila the Hun to stop ravaging Gaul*
This morning the relics of Felix and Projectus

were carried from the abbot's office to the church by a great procession of monks in a cloud of incense fumes and the smoke from a thousand candles. The procession wound around the abbey grounds and into the church, where we all waited. After Mass, the abbot blessed us and we were allowed to come to the altar to kiss the holy relics. When it was my turn, I found that Felix and Projectus were two tiny glass jars of dust, set into large gold and jewel-encrusted holders. Felix's jar was much fuller; he must have been the taller brother. I said a prayer, asking the Roman brothers to help me get free of Shaggy Beard, and then we left for home.

30TH DAY OF JULY, *Feast of Saint Tatwin, archbishop of Canterbury and maker of riddles*

At dinner I saw my aunt Ethelfritha whisper something to George. He patted her fondly on her sleeve and smiled. My heart fell to my stomach, I was so distressed to see him love someone not me. But then I rejoiced to see him smile again. Thank you, God. Bless my aunt Ethelfritha and strike me dumb before I ever meddle with love again.

31ST DAY OF JULY, *Feast of Saint Germanus, the only saint I know who was a lawyer*

Tomorrow is Lammas. Harvest is near. My mother grows larger every day. I will not consent.

<h1>AUGUST ✠</h1>

1ST DAY OF AUGUST, *Lammas Day and Feast of Saint Ethelwold, monk, cook, and builder of the largest organ in England*

This day the church smelled much like the bread stall at a fair from all the fresh-baked loaves brought in thanks to God for the good harvest. Since I had no breakfast, the smells made my mouth water and my stomach rumble like an ox-cart on a rutty road.

After Mass we feasted in the hall. Of the many dishes my favorites were the eel pie and the ginger wafers. My least favorite was the swan's neck pudding.

2ND DAY OF AUGUST, *Feast of Saint Sidwell, virgin, who died when her jealous stepmother incited the reapers to behead her*

In the meadow the other day, I noticed how the trees stand bowed over, looking like old men with heavy burdens on their backs, hunched with worry.

But what might a tree worry about? Mayhap about the young birds who are born amidst its branches and then fly out into the world where they could be caught by cats, stoned by boys, or snared and eaten, and never even say goodbye? About hot, dry summers and thirsty roots that cannot call for water and are never offered beer? About whether its leaves will turn fiery shades of red and gold for all to admire or just shrivel and drop or be blown off by early wind and rain? About being cut down to make a house or a barn or, worse, siege weapons for war or a battering ram? About being chosen to hang a thief whose body would be left there to hang like putrid fruit and no young girl would lie beneath its branches and look up and wonder? Would I could ask one.

4TH DAY OF AUGUST, *Feast of Saint Sithney. God asked him to be the patron saint of girls but Sithney said he'd rather be the patron of mad dogs, so he is. I like to think of him as my father's special saint*

My father returned today unexpectedly. There was no supper to his liking, so he kicked at the dogs and slapped the servers and bellowed, "Sweet Satan, why am I cursed with a cook who labors long in the kitchen yet produces nothing but farts and belches?"

I thought it was quite funny, but I laughed behind my hand. All is quiet now.

9TH DAY OF AUGUST, *Feast of Saint Romanus, Roman doorkeeper and martyr*

My mother lies sore afflicted with a fever. I can write no more.

10TH DAY OF AUGUST, *Feast of Saint Laurence, who was roasted over hot coals and now is the patron saint of cooks. Sometimes religion is as mysterious as love*
Her fever still rages.

13TH DAY OF AUGUST, *Feast of Saint Cassian, a severe schoolmaster who was stabbed to death by his pupils with their pen nibs. I will add this to my list of ways for Shaggy Beard to die*
My mother is finally well, thanks be to God, and still carries the child. I might be made to marry by force, but I vow no one could make me have a child! Not only is it dangerous and uncomfortable, the child could grow into Robert. Or Geoffrey. Or Attila the Hun.

The beast my father has been even beastlier these days when my mother lay ill—at least with me and Morwenna and the servants. He is like a lamb with my mother, or at least a dog or a squirrel or some other gentler beast. God's thumbs! When he does not roar, I do not know who he is. Or just why I hate him.

15TH DAY OF AUGUST, *Feast of Saint Tarsicius, a Roman boy beaten to death with stones and clubs while protecting the Holy Bread*
My mother has been ill again, and I have given

over my days and most of my nights to nursing her. Sometimes I feel that she is the child and I the mother, as I bathe her face and sing her songs and cajole her into eating just a bit of this meat or that cheese.

In one week we go to Herringford to the fair, and for the first time I can remember she will not be with us.

22ND DAY OF AUGUST, *Feast of Saint Alexander of Alexandria, who died a martyr after suffering numerous agonies from scrapers and whips*

It is Bartlemas Fair, easily the busiest and merriest days of the summer. After days of preparation, we left the manor gay and giddy and ready for play. And today we are here.

Before I left her, my mother gave me ten pence for spending. I bought her a string of jet beads—3 pennies, a wooden whistle for Perkin—2 pennies, a bone rattle for the coming babe—1 penny, and four skins of parchment for my herbal—4 pennies. In one morning, all my money gone.

Still, I have yet to eat my fill of pork and pastries, cheer the fastest horses and the fleetest runners, wonder at the tumblers and magicians, laugh at the puppets and giants, and clap for every dancer and minstrel at the fair.

We are at an inn tonight in a room with seven people and seven thousand fleas.

I used to think the saddest sight in the world was an eagle I once saw in a baron's hall, wings clipped, chained to a perch from which it kept falling, flapping piteously until someone righted it again. But there is worse. Here at the fair is a dancing bear, moth-eaten and scrawny, anxious only to be taken home and fed and not prodded and pinched to do silly tricks for fairgoers.

The performance I saw was so clumsy and sad and brought the bear's owner so little profit that he announced a bearbaiting, planning to set a pack of dogs against the poor bear and see who cries and bleeds and dies first, all for the amusement of those wagering money on the outcome. How can we think ourselves made in the likeness of God when we act worse than beasts?

While Morwenna was pondering over willow bowls and iron pots, I argued with the bear's owner, trying to make him see the wrong in sacrificing a bear whose only crime is not wanting to dance for strangers. Finally he said, grinning, he would sell me the bear and I could do what I wished with it. There is the pouch of silver from Shaggy Beard, but if I use it to save the bear, I am chained to *both* beasts. Spending the silver will mean my consent. It will be a promise to God. I can be sly and crafty and false with my father and my suitors, but I fear to fool with God. What can I do?

24TH DAY OF AUGUST, *Feast of Saint Bartholomew, apostle, skinned alive. Patron of butchers, skinners, tanners, leatherworkers, and bookbinders*

Corpus bones! I have talked to every rich or poor, young or old, fat or scrawny merchant at the fair, trying to persuade them that a dancing bear would improve their business, increase their earnings, and bring them great renown. They laughed at me, pushed me, pinched me, tickled me, tried to kiss and fondle and even tumble me, but no one listened to me. No one wants the bear, but I can not abandon him to the cruelty of men and dogs. The bearbaiting is set for tomorrow. What am I to do?

25TH DAY OF AUGUST, *Feast of Saint Ebbe, an abbess who allowed her nuns to spend their time weaving fine clothes, adorning themselves like brides, and neglecting vigils and prayers. Would I could find a nunnery like that*

I have done it. I have promised the silver toothpick and half my pouch of silver in trade for the bear. I know that by accepting his gifts, I have accepted the giver, and I am Shaggy Beard's. For the sake of the bear, I am resigned. Deus help me, but what else could I do?

The owner has agreed to keep him for seven days while I fetch the silver from home and think on what to do with a bear. I would choose to let him live free in the woods and fields, but I know no village that would take kindly to a bear roaming its woods. Mayhap I can convince my father to keep him. He is gentle and good (the bear, not my father) and will hurt no one. He can sleep in the cow barn and I will share my food with him.

26TH DAY OF AUGUST, *Feast of Saint Ninian, apostle to the blue-painted Picts*

We are home again. It dispirits me to think with what high hopes I went to the fair and how I have come home bound to marry a stranger with a scraggy beard and meat caught between his teeth. I am dispirited, downcast, and dejected.

I have asked everyone here to help me fetch and keep the bear. My father refused to talk about it. My mother turned pale. Morwenna humphed and scolded. Perkin sighed and looked the other way. I am surrounded by unfeeling dolts and idiots. Then the largest dolt and idiot of all joined in. Robert came home. He teased me, saying mayhap I could marry the bear since I seem to like them big and hairy and stupid.

The harvest is finished. The villagers brought in the last sheaf with their usual merriment and the whole village joined us for a harvest supper in the hall. I had no appetite. Instead I sulked and wept, slapped Morwenna and was slapped right back, kicked my father in the leg and Peppercorn in her tail, and was sent from the hall in disgrace. My mother came later to my chamber and tried to talk gently to me about dignity and duty and obedience. She said I put her in mind of a beast in a cage, hurling and pounding its poor body against bars that will not give. I listened meekly, but my whole self shudders at the thought of belonging to the despicable Shaggy Beard.

Thinking on it, I feel much like this bear. We can neither of us live alone and free and survive in this world, but we might wish for a cage less painful and confining. Deus help us both.

27TH DAY OF AUGUST, *Feast of Saint Decuman, a Welsh monk beheaded while at prayer*

William Steward told me of an abbey west of here whose abbess keeps a menagerie—lions and wolves and eagles. Would that she might take my bear! I begged William to ride to her, but he cannot leave the manor. Nor Perkin nor Sym. My father will not. Thomas and Edward are away. Robert rode off this evening looking for mischief. I have only five days in which to solve this.

28TH DAY OF AUGUST, *Feast of Saint Augustine of Hippo, who was a rake and a drunkard before he was touched by God and became a saint and a writer of boring holy books*

No one will help me. I argued again with my father. I said I would wed Shaggy Beard if he would keep the bear. He said I would wed Shaggy Beard and to Hell with the bear! I stamped my feet, he cracked me, I said I was going to the abbey, he locked me in my chamber. God's thumbs. Our every meeting ends the same way.

30TH DAY OF AUGUST, *Feast of Saint Fiacre, a hermit who hated women but loved plants*

I am still locked away, still helpless. What will happen to the bear?

31ST DAY OF AUGUST, *Feast of Saints Quenburga and Cuthburga, sisters and nuns*

My mother has been here. She said: "He whom you call abominable rode all night to the abbey by the sea. He charmed the abbess into taking your bear. They sent a wagon and two men to the fair to trade your silver for the beast. In thanks, Robert also gave the abbess silver—his own. You are to stay in your chamber and think on this."

So the bear is safe! Thanks to Robert. Robert? This is not the brother I know. I am confounded.

September ✠

1ST DAY OF SEPTEMBER, *Feast of Saint Giles, patron of cripples, lepers, nursing mothers, and blacksmiths*

More lady-lessons. I let my mother instruct me but once I leave her I plan to do as I please. The pig who wishes to wed me liked me well enough when I did not walk with my eyes cast down and hands clasped. God's thumbs! If he doesn't like me to grab up my skirts and run, he can send me back. Oh that he would!

THE HOUR OF VESPERS, LATER THIS DAY: I once had a nightmare that I was lost in the woods in the fog and I could not find my way out and I could hear a boar rutting in the bushes, coming closer and closer. When I woke, I found it was no dream but true and I was lost in the woods. This day is like that. I have been walking in a bad dream since

Robert's wedding when the pig first laid his eyes on me, and now I wake to find it is true.

A messenger arrived this noon. Shaggy Beard will be here before September is over. We will be formally betrothed and will ride north together to be married in the church at Lithgow. I accepted his silver. I consented. The bear is safe and I am doomed.

2ND DAY OF SEPTEMBER, *Feast of Saint Stephen of Hungary, a king who commanded all his subjects to marry*

My father rode to London yesterday but will not be gone long, wanting to be back before the baby is born. My mother is so thin and frail to heave her heavy load around. If it would not make her sad, I would wish this baby away.

4TH DAY OF SEPTEMBER, *Feast of Saint Ultan, who founded a school, educated and fed poor students, illuminated manuscripts, and wrote a life of Saint Brigid*

My mother has labored for two days to birth her child but it will not come. Morwenna is with her now. She sent me to rest but rest I cannot while my mother suffers so.

Her torment began Sunday morn when all were in church except my sleeping mother and me left to tend her. Suddenly her pains began. I comforted her as best I could and then ran for someone to send to old Nan from the village. Nan drinks and stinks and stumbles but her babies mostly live.

Everyone was still at Mass, except for Odd William snoring by the fire like a pig in the sun. I woke him roughly and told him how to find Nan. He refused to go, saying he was just writing of how the great King Arthur led the Britons against the barbarian invaders and was not at a stopping place. Corpus bones! I slapped him so hard I spilled his ink but still he sat by the fire talking of the dead Arthur while my living mother labored upstairs. The knotty-pated, clay-brained clodpole!

I went back to my mother and sang and bathed her face until Mass was over and the manor came alive again and old Nan could be fetched.

My mother labored all day and night and day and night again with no result, but this morning we could see the top of a tiny head. Nan, fearing for the child's life, baptized it while the rest of it stays stuck in my mother. Although I made her a drink of wallflowers in warm wine and untied all the knots and unstopped all the jugs in the manor, no more of the child has come forth yet and I am terribly afraid. Dear Saint Margaret, who watches over women in childbirth, help my mother. She is gentle and good and does the best that she can with the beast my father and her difficult children.

5TH DAY OF SEPTEMBER, *Feast of Saint Bertin, French abbot and farmer*

Our baby was born last evening, a dear beautiful scrawny little girl. I cleaned the spittle from her mouth and the blood from her body, wrapped her in clean linen, and laid her next my mother, who wept from joy and exhaustion.

Since then my mother suffers greatly with a fever. I rubbed her back with an ointment of wild poppy and oil of violets and gave her some in a goblet of honeyed wine. She rests now.

The baby sleeps in a cradle near my bed and I pretend she is mine. I have hung garlic and rowan about the cradle to ward off witches and am watching her closely to make sure she breathes. She does. She lives.

6TH DAY OF SEPTEMBER, *I don't know whose day this is*

My mother's fever is worse. O dear Saint Margaret, who cares for women in childbed, dear Blessed Virgin, most especially dear God, please save my mother! Nan has gone back to the village, saying there is nothing more she could do, but I will not stop trying. Morwenna and I bathe her face with cool linen and pour goblets of wine down her parched throat. We have stopped all the windows and built up the fire but still her fever rages.

7TH DAY OF SEPTEMBER

I do not know how she can be so hot and not consume herself and the bed linen and the whole manor in flames. I have not slept nor Morwenna since the baby was born. Bess from the kitchen has taken her and feeds her with the same milk and the same love she feeds her own babe. Dear God, I can do no more for either of them. Morwenna will not let me back in my mother's chamber until I rest and eat, so I am pretending to do so while really I write this and pray.

8TH DAY OF SEPTEMBER, *Birth of the Virgin Mary*

My mother worsened and we sent for Father Huw to ease her dying. And then my father came home.

He threw Father Huw down the stairs, opened the window in the solar, cast all of us out, and stayed there with her pacing and whispering and shouting until dark. He came out then, face gray but eyes shining, to say she lives. And will live. I thank you, God, and the Virgin Mary, whose birthday this is, and my father, the most unlikely agent of a miracle that I know. I think he just battled the devil and won.

9TH DAY OF SEPTEMBER, *Feast of Saint Ciaran of Clonmacnoise, an Irish abbot who used a fox to carry his papers until it ate them*

She still lives. And the baby also. My mother demanded that the cradle be moved back into her chamber, so I have made a bed on the floor near them. I must keep them safe. We will call the baby Eleanor Mary Catherine.

10TH DAY OF SEPTEMBER, *Feast of Saint Frithestan, bishop of Winchester*

Now that I am about to leave, I feel how dear this place is to me. I sat in the field next to the village this morning, trying to memorize the sounds—the squeal of cart wheels and the bawling of babies, the shouts of children and peddlers and cross old women, the hissing of the geese and the roosters' crow. The dogs were barking, the water wheel splashed, and the smith's hammer rang like a church bell. I took it all into my heart so I can play it like music whenever I need to.

11TH DAY OF SEPTEMBER, *Feast of Saints Protus and Hyacinth, brothers and slaves, who were burned alive*

I am painting on my chamber wall God holding baby Eleanor in his arms. What I think about God is that He is not some old white-haired man. If God can be anything He wants, why would He choose to be an old man? Thomas Baker's grandfather is an old man; he has no teeth and coughs and spits painfully. John Over-Bridge is an old man. He hobbles from his house to the woods to piss and is barely able to hobble home. I think God would not choose to be an old man. Or a woman—God's father would probably marry Him off to some pig in pants. No, I think God is like a young king, clean and shining in his armor, with long legs and soft eyes, mounted on a white horse, singing and smiling. And that is how He is on my chamber wall.

12TH DAY OF SEPTEMBER, *Feast of Saint Ailbe, an Irish bishop who was suckled by a wolf*

I am excited, saddened, and confused. I cannot

talk to Aelis about this, for it is she who confuses me. We met in the meadow this morning. I waited there until the sun was high and a thousand new spots popped out on my nose before she finally arrived. Her color was bright and her breathing labored, and not just from the heat and the climb, it appears. Her father has told her she is to wed my brother Robert!

I fell upon her in tears, babbling about how we were in the same barrel of pickles and could run away together and give puppet shows at fairs and to Hell with Shaggy Beard and his silver and my promise. Aelis just laughed and put her hand over my mouth.

"Hush your chirping, Little Bird," she said. "Wedding Robert is my idea."

Then she sang on about his shining eyes and strong hands and lusty laugh. Robert! She must have been enchanted by some witch with a mind to jests. Robert! I tried to tell her of his abominations and his utter beastliness but her cheeks grew pink and she laughed and said, "Yes, I know, Robert is a true man." God's thumbs! Robert!

So I am excited that Aelis will be my sister, saddened because I will not be here to enjoy her but will be prisoner to some pig in the north who sends his bride a toothpick and a sewing kit. But mostly I am confused. Why would Aelis marry Robert? What about George, whom she vowed to love until she died? And who is Robert, the beast I see or the lover

Aelis sees? The rascal he acts or the young man who found a home for a shabby bear to please his little sister? I think sometimes that people are like onions. On the outside smooth and whole and simple but inside ring upon ring, complex and deep.

13TH DAY OF SEPTEMBER, *Feast of Saint John Chrysostom, archbishop of Constantinople, killed by enforced travel in bad weather*

I sought Robert after dinner and asked if he weren't still grieving over his poor dead wife and their babe and how could he think to wed again so soon. He told me to keep my beak out of his business and grinned. He has lost a front tooth. Good.

Today I finished painting baby Eleanor's face on the mural in my chamber. Mayhap when she grows older, it will be her chamber and she will think on the sister who lived and slept and painted here.

Only five days to Shaggy Beard.

14TH DAY OF SEPTEMBER, *the return of the True Cross to Jerusalem by the emperor Heraclius of Judea*

We gathered nuts today—walnuts, chestnuts, hazelnuts, looking especially for the double nuts that protect against rheumatism and the spells of witches. As we gathered, I imagined eating them, in sauces and cakes and roasted in the fire on a stormy November night. I cannot believe I will not be here to share them.

Four days until Shaggy Beard.

15TH DAY OF SEPTEMBER, *Feast of Saint Adam, bishop of Scotland, who was burned to death by his people for increasing the tax on cows*

Three days to Shaggy Beard.

My mother let me look today in her mirror of polished silver. "I must know how I look right now," I told her. "I must see myself as myself once more before I become the unwilling Lady Shaggy Beard." She unwrapped the disk from its velvet covers and held it before me. My eyes are still gray, not blue, and my hair brown, not gold. The sunspots are still there, dotting my nose and cheeks like speckles on an egg, though my mother says I look none so bad when I am not squinting or sulking.

16TH DAY OF SEPTEMBER, *Feast of Saint Edith, virgin, whose thumb remained uncorrupted after death*

I have the opinion that longing to be blue-eyed and golden-haired like the maidens in songs profits me nothing. Easier, I think, to change the songs than my face. So I have begun a new song:

Her eyes were gray and brown her hair
As she went down to Bartlemas Fair.
With her rumpled clothes
And spotted nose
No blue-eyed beauty could compare.

I will finish it some other day.

17TH DAY OF SEPTEMBER, *Feast of Saint Francis of Assisi receiving the five wounds of Christ*

Morwenna and I have packed my gowns and robes this day. I have wandered the manor since, saying goodbye to the barn cats and the chickens, to Perkin's goats and Sym's pigs, to Meg in the dairy and Gerd at the mill and Rhys in the stables. When I reached the dovecote, the doves put me in mind of myself, raised only to breed and to die. So I let them out and shooed them away. I have no doubt they will come back—doves are none too bright—but for now they are free.

And I let my chamber birds go as well, taking each to the window and wishing it Godspeed as I opened the cage door. Goodbye to Dittany and Clubmoss, Wormwood, Saffron, Sage, and all the others. I who must be caged could leave them no longer in cages. So I set them free—all but the popinjay, who could not survive on his own. I gave him to Perkin, as well as the other half of my pouch of silver so he can buy his way free from his obligations to my father and find a way to become a scholar. I have no doubt he will do it. Perkin is still the cleverest person I know.

One day to Shaggy Beard.

21ST DAY OF SEPTEMBER, *Feast of Saint Matthew, apostle and evangelist, martyred in Ethiopia. Or Persia*

The day after I last wrote, riders from Shaggy

Beard appeared at our hall. While they were closed away with my father, I ran to the high meadow to say goodbye to Perkin. When I reached the road, however, instead of crossing over, I turned north. I was fairly crazed with fear, like a beast pursued by dogs, thinking only to get away. Then I saw a picture in my mind of my aunt Ethelfritha winking and telling me to run to her next time. By cock and pie, I thought, I will do it! Uncle George I am not sure of, but Aunt Ethelfritha will help me! I tucked a sprig of mugwort in my shoe so I should not tire on the journey and set off for York.

I was two days on that road and mugwort or no mugwort arrived looking like a dying duck in a thunderstorm. I had taken not a penny nor a crust and I was afraid to be seen, so I dared not ask for food. My stomach worm gnawed all the way to York. I slept outside in haystacks and, thanks be, had no rain until the last afternoon. By the time I arrived yestereve just after supper I was so hungry and weary and footsore I could not walk an ace farther.

My uncle George was from home for the night but there was my dear aunt Ethelfritha, a little more broad across the narrow but merry and warm. She put me in mind of Morwenna, for she made me wash and comb my hair before she would let me eat. If she had said, "Have some cheese. It will keep your bowels open," I would have sworn it *was* Morwenna. Finally she fed me with herring pie left from supper and a parsnip pudding while I told her my troubles.

We huddled in her great bed until very late making plans for my deliverance. "Ireland," she said first. "Across the water to Ireland where sure there are relatives of your lady mother who will hide and protect you."

Ireland seemed no easy escape to me so I proposed London, where I might make my way by . . . what? Embroidering? Hemming sheets? Brewing remedies for ale head and swollen legs?

No Ireland. No London. We fell asleep still unsettled. Before dawn I was awakened by a screech and a face full of chin whiskers right next to mine. Ethelfritha.

"Of course," the face bellowed. "Cathay! George must know merchants who trade there. We could disguise you as a slave girl being sent as a gift to the great khan and carry you muffled in veils on the back of a camel. The trip is three years over snowy mountains and blazing deserts so for certain no one would find you there.

"Or dancing girls," she cried. "We are slim and supple dancing girls from some Saracen court where we bewitch the sultan with our beauty. Or I will ask my sons the king, the pope, and Saint Peter to help us . . ." and she was off somewhere on her own, no longer Ethelfritha but some personage of her own making.

God's thumbs! My aunt Ethelfritha is as mad as the moon! She had forgotten herself again just when I needed her. I could see she would be no help. I was alone in my troubles and I alone had to conceive a plan before George came home so I could convince him it would be worth the trouble to help me.

Sitting beneath a pear tree later in the drizzling rain, I thought about my choices. I have no desire for three years of snowy mountains or some Saracen court. I cannot be a monk shut off from the world. I cannot be a crusader riding over the bloody bodies of strangers I am supposed to hate, or a wandering minstrel unconnected to any place or anybody. I cannot be like Odd William, involved only with the dead people he writes about while the living swirl in joy and pain around him. I cannot be like Aunt Ethelfritha, who, in being anyone she chooses, forgets who she really is.

Suddenly I saw the old Jewish woman saying, "Remember, Little Bird, in the world to come, you will not be asked 'Why were you not George?' or 'Why were you not Perkin?' but 'Why were you not Catherine?'" And it came into my head that I cannot run away. I am who I am wherever I am.

Like the bear and my popinjay, I cannot survive by myself. But I also cannot survive if I am not myself. And who am I? I am no minstrel and no wart charmer but me, Birdy, Catherine of Stonebridge, daughter of Lord Rollo and the lady Aislinn, sister to Robert and Thomas and Edward and little Eleanor, friend of Perkin, goat boy and scholar.

I am like the Jews in our hall, driven from England, from one life to another, and yet for them exile was no exile. Wherever they go, they take their lives, their families, their people, and their God with them, like a light that never goes out. I imagine them somewhere in Flanders eating their Jewish food and talking their horses' talk and loving one another and their God. At home even in exile.

Just so, my family and Perkin and Meg and Gerd and Aelis and the barn cats and even my father are part of me, and I part of them, so even in my new life I will not be far from home.

I realize that Shaggy Beard has won my body, but no matter whose wife I am, I will still be me. Mayhap I can do what I must and still be me, still survive and, please God, even thrive. I have girded my loins like a warrior from the Bible and am going forth to do battle with the enemy. He shall not find it a comfortable prize he has won, this gray-eyed, sun-browned beauty. Amen.

After dinner my uncle George came home, surprised but pleased to see me. His mouth smiled and his eyes almost did as I told him of the mad plans of Ethelfritha and how I decided I cannot escape my life but can only use my determination and courage to make it the best I can. He will take me home tomorrow. We will ride, which suits my feet just fine.

22ND DAY OF SEPTEMBER, *Feast of Saint Maurice and his six thousand six hundred sixty-six companions, Roman soldiers of the Theban Legion, martyred for refusing to sacrifice to pagan gods*

We leave in one hour. In George's garden I saw a

toad, may it bring me luck. And as Morwenna says, luck is better than early rising.

23RD DAY OF SEPTEMBER, *Feast of Saint Thecla of Iconium, virgin and follower of Saint Paul. Condemned to be burnt, a storm put out the fire. Sent to be eaten by beasts, they would not. She escaped and lived in a cave for seventy-two years*

I am home again. Such ado! I was kissed and slapped and lectured until my ears turned inside out. I told my tale and then sat to listen to theirs.

It seems God is indeed watching over me. Or else toads really are lucky. How I know is this:

The riders from the north did not say that Shaggy Beard comes for his bride, but that he is dead, killed in a brawl over a tavern maid. His son Stephen is now Baron Selkirk, Lord of Lithgow, Smithburn, Random, and Fleece, and wishes to honor the marriage contract in his father's place. He sent me an enameled brooch of a little bird with a pearl in its beak. I am wearing it now.

My lady mother and the beast my father think it no better and no worse that I marry Stephen instead of Shaggy Beard, but for me it is like moving from the darkness into the light, like coming in from a cold gray mist and seeing the fire make a warm and golden glow in the center of the hall, like the yolk of a boiled egg or the deeper gold in the belly of a rose.

As I sit here in my chamber watching the sun set, I realize that the fear that drove me this half year is gone. Shaggy Beard is gone. I think I do not truly even remember what he looked or acted or sounded like. Mayhap Shaggy Beard was never so bad as I imagine him. Or mayhap he was.

In any event, I am, if not free, at least less painfully caged. I am filled with a trembling that feels like feathers fluttering in my gut but I think is hope. All I know of Stephen is that he is young and clean, loves learning, and is not Shaggy Beard. For these alone I am prepared to love him.

I have been making a list of names for our children. I think to call the first one George. Or Perkin. Or Edward. Or Ethelfritha. Or Magpie. Or mayhap Stephen. The world is full of possibilities.

I leave in October. Only one month until Stephen!

Here ends the book of Catherine, called Little Bird or Birdy, of the Manor of Stonebridge in the shire of Lincoln, in the country of England, in the hands of God. Now I leave it to you, Edward, to judge whether this exercise of yours has indeed left me more observant, thoughtful, and learned. God's thumbs!

Author's Note

The England of 1290 is a foreign country. It would seem foreign even to people who have been to England or live there now. Things might look familiar—the same hills and sea and sky. People, young and old, short and tall, wear clothing we could identify and speak a language we might recognize. But their world is different from ours. The difference runs deeper than what they eat or where they bathe or who decides who marries whom. Medieval people live in a place we can never go, made up of what they value, how they think, and what they believe is true and important and possible.

The difference begins with how people saw themselves. Everyone had a particular place in a community, be it village, abbey, manor, family, or guild. Few people considered moving out of their place. Even people's names were linked to their place—Thomas Baker, William Steward, John At-Wood, Murgaw of Lithgow. Perkin, the goat boy who wants to be a scholar, is unusual.

Our ideas of individual identity, individual accomplishments and rights, individual effort and success did not exist. Family and community and guild and country were what mattered. No one was separate and independent, even the king.

This fixture of place was enforced by people's relationship to the land. When William, Duke of Normandy, conquered England in 1066, he decided that all the land belonged to him. He parceled out large estates to his supporters—barons and counts and dukes and great churchmen. They in turn rented smaller sections to abbots and knights, who let even smaller parcels to the farmers and millers and blacksmiths in the villages. Those on the bottom paid rent to those above, who paid it to the king, and everyone owed protection to those below them, making a great circle with everyone connected. The king was in cooperation with the lowest landholder, for the small bits of poor land in the farthest village could be traced back to the king, and the king owed patronage and protection to all his people.

Some great noblemen held many manors with many villages scattered all across England. Some, like Birdy's father, held but one knight's fee—that is, enough land to support one knight and his family, for which the knight owed service or the equivalent in money to his landlord. The villagers then rented parcels from the knight, in exchange for work or goods or money or all three.

Although great lords lived in castles and lesser lords in large manor houses, most English people in 1290 lived in villages, in small cottages lining the road from manor to church. A village might seem like a miniature to us, with perhaps thirty small cottages, tiny front yards full of vegetables and chickens, and the fields cut into strips so each tenant would have some good and some not-so-good land.

Time in these villages moved slowly—not in a line from hour to hour, past to future, but again in a circle, marked by the passing of the seasons, the cycle of church festivals, and yearly village holidays. Daily life was marked by the rising and setting of the sun, for there were no watches or clocks, no gas lamps or electric lights, and candles were expensive and dangerous to use in a house of thatch and wood. Most people did not know what century it was, much less what year.

The future, then, to most medieval English meant not next week or next year or 1300, but the world to come, the afterlife, eternity, Heaven and Hell. Since the Church had a say in who went where in the next life, it had great authority in this one. The Church had power, lands, and riches. Church courts could condemn someone to death for heresy. Blasphemy was not only a sin, but also a crime. Almost everyone loved God and worshipped Him in the same ways at the same times in the same kinds of places. The Church said God hated those who didn't—heathens, heretics, pagans, and Jews—so they were slaughtered in His name. Everyone hoped the world to come would be better than this one.

Children, too, were part of the great circle of life, learning from their elders and passing that knowledge on to their own sons and daughters. Village children lived at home, learning at a young age to help about the cottage or fields, tending animals or those children younger than they. Children in town often were apprenticed to craftsmen or sent to be servants.

Noble children, both boys and girls, were sent to another noble home to be fostered. Once when a visitor from Italy asked why parents sent their children away, he was told, "Children learn better manners in other people's houses."

Boys like Geoffrey served the lord of the manor while they trained to be knights. Girls like Birdy and Aelis went to a wealthy manor, such as Belleford, where they attended the lady of the manor and learned music, sewing, household skills, and manners. They also learned doctoring, since the lady of the manor provided the only medical help most people got. Broken bones, bloody cuts, coughs, and even fatal diseases were treated by the lady with remedies she grew, picked, brewed, and bottled herself. Some herbal remedies were effective, such as the use of poppy flowers to ease pain. Some were not, as when a plant was used for ailments of the heart or liver because its leaf was shaped like a heart or a liver. There were no cures for most illnesses, no treatments for most diseases, no real alternatives to herbs, magic, and luck.

Girls were mostly trained for marriage. Marriage among the noble classes was not a matter of love but of economics. Marriages were arranged to increase land, gain allies, or pay back debts. Women were essentially property, used to further a family's alliances, wealth, or status. Birdy fought years of training and tradition in opposing her marriage to Shaggy Beard. Most girls would have consented, knowing no alternative.

When looked at from a safe, warm, well-fed perspective, the foreign country of medieval England might seem like a place of hard work, cruelty, and dirt. But the English of the Middle Ages also had a fondness for merriment, dancing, crude jokes, and boisterous games. Many households, such as Birdy's, entertained themselves by the fire with riddles, roasted apples, and music. Villagers put aside their hard, tedious lives to dance around the Maypole, jump the bonfires on Midsummer Night, and share Christmas dinner with their lord and lady.

Can we really understand medieval people well enough to write or read books about them? I think we can identify with those qualities that we share— the yearning for a full belly, the need to be warm and safe, the capacity for fear and joy, love for children, pleasure in a blue sky or a handsome pair of eyes. As for the rest, we'll have to imagine and pretend and make room in our hearts for all sorts of different people.

Books that will help young readers learn about medieval England include Joseph and Frances Gies's series *Life in a Medieval City, Life in a Medieval Vil-*

lage, and *Life in a Medieval Castle*; Dorothy Hartley's *Lost Country Life*; Madeleine Pelner Cosman's *Fabulous Feasts: Medieval Cookery and Ceremony*; Marjorie and C. H. B. Quennell's *A History of Everyday Things in England, 1066–1799;* and Alfred Duggan's *Growing Up in Thirteenth Century England.*

Readers who want to get a sense of the Middle Ages from first-hand accounts are directed to Bartholomaeus Anglicus's *On the Properties of Things*; *The Medieval Woman's Guide to Health*; *The Travels of Sir John Mandeville*; *The Babees Book: Medieval Manners for the Very Young;* and Geoffrey Chaucer's *The Canterbury Tales.*

These stories set in or near the Middle Ages may be found at local libraries:

Marchette Chute, *Innocent Wayfaring*

Marguerite De Angeli, *The Door in the Wall*

Elizabeth Janet Gray, *Adam of the Road*

E. L. Konigsburg, *A Proud Taste for Scarlet and Miniver*

Norah Lofts, *The Maude Reed Tale*

Katherine Marcuse, *The Devil's Workshop*

Mary Stolz, *Pangur Ban*

Rosemary Sutcliff, *Knight's Fee* and *The Witch's Brat*

Also from Newbery Medal–winning author Karen Cushman

A girl who knows no home, no parents, nor any name but Beetle makes a home for herself in a tiny village assisting the midwife, a hard woman with a sharp glance and an even sharper temper. When Beetle fails at an important assignment, she runs away. Is Beetle truly a know-nothing who belongs nowhere? Or does the midwife's apprentice have a name and a place in the world?

"A fascinating view of a far distant time."
— *The Horn Book* (starred review)

Winner of the Newbery Medal

Pb 0-06-440630-X

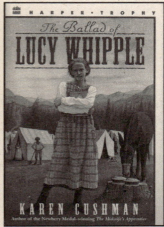

Pb 0-06-440684-9

California doesn't suit Lucy Whipple — not the name, not the place. Lucky Diggins is barely even a town — just a ramshackle of huts and tobacco-spitting miners. There's not even a lending library! But moving out West was her mother's dream. So Lucy vows to be miserable until she can go back East, except that Lucy may be in for a surprise....

"A coming of age story rich with historical flavor."
— *Publishers Weekly* (starred review)

HarperTrophy®
An Imprint of HarperCollinsPublishers
www.harperchildrens.com